THE DOCTOR'S PROMISE

A BILLIONAIRE ROMANCE

MICHELLE LOVE

CONTENTS

Made in "The United States" by:

Michelle Love

© Copyright 2021

ISBN: 978-1-64808-844-5

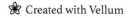 Created with Vellum

society families, was entirely the opposite of who Noemi had expected her to be. Rather than taking advantage of her family's position and vast wealth, Thomasina—Tomi—worked tirelessly for underprivileged kids in Seattle's poorer neighborhoods. Noemi and she had bonded immediately, both sharing a goofy sense of humor. Thomasina had been fascinated by Noemi's story: a mixed-race kid adopted by a middle-class white family who had repaid their love and kindness by being a straight-A student and paying her own way through college and med school.

Now, having reached the position of surgical resident in cardiology, her favorite specialty, Noemi's career was just taking off. Of course, her personal life was another matter. What personal life? she would often say to herself. She had dated Dieter briefly when she had first joined Sacred Heart Seattle, but she soon learned the cardiology resident was arrogant and only interested in her because she had been the shining star of her class at Stanford.

Her real joy here was her mentor; Lazlo Merchant, Chief of Surgery and a cardio God, had taken Noemi under his wing, and he was like a surrogate father to her. He was certainly her champion, pushing her farther than the rest of the residents. Lazlo was also the sweetest man, and Noemi adored him.

Now, she checked Thomasina's charts. "I'm supposed to be asking you how you are doing, Tomi." She looked around. "Rafa not here?"

"He went to take Bepi to my mom's. Bepi's being fussy, wanting his dad to read to him if I can't be there." Bepi was Thomasina's two-year-old son, an adorable curly-headed young boy. Bepi's father, Thomasina's fiancée, was object of a crush for every female in the hospital. Tall, dark, and devastatingly handsome, Rafael Genova was a quiet, thoughtful man who adored his fiancée and their son. Though a CEO of an international shipping company, the Italian billionaire was strangely shy. With Thomasina being the life and soul of any party, Noemi supposed, Rafa didn't need to do anything but let her take the lead.

Becoming close to Thomasina, however, didn't preclude Noemi from finding Rafa sinfully attractive. He was gorgeous—all dark curls and bright green eyes. His smile, though rarely seen, lit up any room. Noemi could tell he was desperately worried about Thomasina, even if Tomi herself laughed off her condition, joking around that she'd have to find Rafa a new fiancée before she 'kicked the bucket.'

"Not going to happen," Noemi would reassure them both with a mock-glare at Tomi. "Not on my watch."

There were a few occasions when Tomi was sleeping with Rafa sitting by her side, that Noemi would see his pain and seek to comfort him, reassure him—but it wasn't her place to do it.

Thomasina watched Noemi as she checked her vitals. "Noe, tell me, honestly. What are the chances of me getting a heart? Really?"

"As good as anyone's. You're at the top of the list now."

"Which means I'm hovering on the verge of croaking."

Noemi shook her head. "It just means you're meeting the criteria UNOS set out."

"And that means I'm really sick. I need you to be honest, doc."

Noemi sighed and sat on the edge of the bed. "Tomi... Yes. You're really sick, or we wouldn't be here. I can't say definitively that you'll get a heart, but by God, I'm praying you do. It's an odd thing to say because it means someone else dying, and that offends all my good intentions. I can't be biased, but I promise you this: the second we get that call from UNOS, I'll harvest the organ myself, and I won't let it out of my sight until it's pumping in your chest."

Thomasina smiled at her. "I could get quite the crush on you, Dr. Castor."

"Ha, right back at you, sister. Now, get some sleep. Doc's orders."

NOEMI SHRUGGED into her denim jacket as she walked out of the hospital. A fine mist of rain was falling, and the November night was bitterly cold. Noemi shivered as the breeze whipped around her. She walked briskly to her car, an ancient Volkswagen with intermittent heating and a rattle that Noemi ignored. She got in and tried to start the ignition. It faltered twice then died. "Oh, no, not now..." She tried again, but the car was dead. "Fuck, fuck, fuckety fuck," she

BLURB

Noemi

It was my fault that his fiancée died...
That's what I keep telling myself. Yes, the car accident wasn't my
fault, but...

Now Rafael Genova is back in my life, and I can't stop thinking
about him.
His eyes.
His dark, brooding gorgeous looks.
...his body.
Every single cell of me reacts when he's near.
My nipples harden, and the pulse between my legs beats so hard I
feel I could cum there and then...
And his lips...
I want him so badly I can taste it, and the way he looks at me...
I think he wants me too.
I hope he wants me as badly as I need him inside me...

∼

Rafael

I never thought I'd love again.
After I lost my fiancée, my entire focus has been on my son.
Except...
Noemi Castor is haunting my dreams.
Her sweet face, her soft hair...
Her curvy lush body...
I get hard just thinking about her in my arms, in my bed, my cock
buried deep inside her, the way her face glows when she cums...
I need her so badly it hurts.
But she won't stop blaming herself for this tragedy in our past.
I'm falling in love with her—this beautiful, funny, sexy girl.
I just have to convince her that I'm crazy about her...

CHAPTER ONE

No matter how many times Doctor Noemi Castor scrubbed in for a surgery, she never lost the thrill of the unknown, the challenge. She looked over at her colleague—her ex-boyfriend—Dieter Flynn and wondered if he felt the same way.

Of course, Dieter had a God Complex, a trait Noemi had always disliked. For her, the challenge was helping the person before them on the operating table, not acquiring surgical bragging rights, but she knew she was the exception, not the rule, in the world of surgery.

"You ready to rock, Noe?" Ally Roberts, her favorite scrub nurse and her best friend, grinned at her, and Noemi nodded.

"Stephen all set? I hope he's not too nervous." Noemi peered in through the viewing window. Their patient, a fifty-five-year-old man, had been waiting for a heart and lung transplant for three years, but had a crippling fear of surgery. Noemi had carefully reassured him that she would do everything to make sure he came though safely.

She heard Dieter make a disgusted noise. "Who cares? Dude will be out for the count anyway." He pushed his way into the theater while Noemi shared an eyeroll with Ally.

"Remind me again why I ever ever dated that guy?"

Ally snorted. "A psychotic break, I'd say. Come on, Super Doc, your patient awaits."

LATER, Noemi sat with Stephen in recovery, and when he awoke, she smiled at him. "Hey, slugger. You did good."

"It went well?" Stephen whispered, soft and raspy.

"Perfectly. Now, your job is to make sure those organs don't reject you, to wine and dine them with the best food this hospital can provide—which isn't saying much, I know—and to sweet talk them with your meds. Can you do that for me?"

Stephen, who she knew harbored a crush on her, grinned at her. "Sure thing, doc. And thank you… I mean it."

She squeezed his hand. "When your vitals are more stable, I'll allow visitors. Muriel is in the waiting room. She won't say it, but I know she's relieved." Muriel was Stephen's fearsome wife, who would never confess she was worried, but had spent the past few hours knitting furiously. When Noemi stepped out to update her that Stephen was okay, her relief was palpable, and she'd even hugged Noemi— which was very out of character.

NOEMI WENT to the changing room and stripped out of her scrubs. It was late, almost ten, and she was ravenously hungry, but before she left the hospital, she stopped in on another patient.

Thomasina Ballentine was awake and reading, and she greeted Noemi happily. "Hey, kiddo, how are you doing?"

She was only five years older than Noemi's twenty-eight, but because of her society position and her effortless grace and poise, Noemi always regarded Thomasina like a much older sister. The tall, willowy, delicately beautiful blonde had been admitted when she got too sick to be at home—her heart, damaged by a seemingly innocent bout of what turned out to be pneumonia, was failing, the result of an undiagnosed condition she'd had from birth.

Thomasina, the daughter of one of Seattle's most prominent

muttered, then jumped violently as someone rapped on her window.

Rafa Genova smiled at her as she rolled the window down. Yes, her car was old enough to have manual windows. "Hey, Noemi... trouble?"

"I'm good with hearts, Rafa, but not with cars."

He laughed softly. "Let me have a look. Pop the hood, would you?"

Noemi watched him as he checked out the engine, seemingly oblivious to the rain. His dark curls stuck to his face as his hair got soaked through, and a small curl of desire warmed Noemi's stomach.

Stop it. He's Tomi's man, and you love Tomi. Stop it.

Noemi looked away as Rafa stood back at up. "It's completely dead, I'm afraid. I could try to jump-start you, but I'm not sure you'd make it all the way home."

"Oh, darn it. Well, I guess it's the bus for me then. Thanks anyway, Rafa. I do appreciate it."

"Nonsense, I'll drive you home. We can arrange for your car to be picked up too."

Noemi shook her head. "No, honestly, you've been kind enough."

But he wouldn't take no for an answer. He called his assistant as they walked back to his Mercedes and arranged for her car to be towed to an auto shop.

Rafa drove her home. Luckily, she didn't live very far from the hospital, so she didn't feel too badly for taking him away from Tomi. He asked her how Thomasina was doing.

"She's in good spirits, Rafa, and she finally ate an entire meal. That's a really good sign. It means she's getting stronger. Any little step like that means she's more likely to survive a transplant."

Rafael nodded. "I know you can't answer this, but..."

"The chances of getting a heart are what they are, Rafa."

"I know," he said softly, and her heart ached for him.

"Is Bepi okay?"

"He's asking a lot of questions about his mom. I keep saying she's going to be okay, but it's getting to the point where I can't lie to him."

"You're not lying to him, Rafa. He's two."

For a long time Rafa was silent before he looked over at her. "What if we lose her, Noemi? Then what do I tell my son?"

Her throat closed, and she shook her head. "I can't answer that for you, Rafa. I have never lost anyone that close."

"I'm glad."

"I wish I could advise you... Look, let's not dwell on that—positive thoughts and all that."

Rafa smiled, and her stomach flipped. She looked away. "You mean," he said, "that you doctors believe in karma? That old cliché?"

"Hell, yes! We'll take anything like that!" she retorted, and they both laughed.

At her apartment building, she thanked him. "You're a lifesaver."

"Least I could do. Goodnight, Noe."

"Goodnight, Rafa."

IN THE MORNING, she found a set of keys pushed through her door mail slot with a note: A loaner for as long as you need it. R.

Outside, a brand-new silver Lexus was parked next to the curb.

2

_____

CHAPTER TWO

"Obviously I can't accept it." Even as Noemi talked to her sister Leonora on the phone, she was sliding into the driver's seat. She groaned. "Oh, God, Leo... so comfy."

Her sister—adopted sister—laughed. "Yeah, you're a goner. How does it feel to be driving a real car?"

"I'll have you know Penelope has been a loyal friend to me."

"You named your piece of junk Volkswagen Penelope?"

Noemi grinned. "And I would name this little beauty... um... Agamemnon."

Leonora laughed. "You are quite insane, sis. Listen, I know you've answered this before, but you did remember to take some vacation the weekend of Dad's birthday, right? No sudden emergency surgeries? He's only seventy-five once."

Her sister's voice carried a warning: Cancel and incur my wrath. Noemi smiled. "All vacation is approved," she said in a robotic voice. "Orders have been followed."

She heard Leonora's half-amused, half-exasperated sigh. "Good. Then I won't have to kill you."

"Talking of people to kill, I have to get to work, so I'll speak to you later."

. . .

NOEMI STEERED the car through the early morning Seattle traffic. Outside, dark clouds packed the sky and the wind was freezing cold and unrelenting. She would call Rafael and thank him when she got to work, but there was no way she could accept this gift, even if it was only a loaner. What a sweet guy. Noemi was still smiling to herself when her phone buzzed again. She pulled the car over when she saw it was a 911.

Dieter was on the phone. "Noe, where are you?"

She told him.

"Good. You need to get over to Tacoma right now. UNOS called. They have a heart for Thomasina Ballentine."

"You're kidding?" Her own heart leaped. "Really?"

"Really... and the helicopter is out of service because of the storm. You're nearest."

"I'm on my way."

Oh, thank God, thank God. Rafael, this is the karma you made fun of last night... Smiling, Noemi turned the car around and sped out of the city towards Tacoma.

TWO HOURS later and she was stepping back into the car, her precious cargo strapped into the seat beside her. The hospital had been surprised when she turned up in her own car, not in an official vehicle, but luckily, Noemi not only had her medical credentials with her, but the cardio attending had given her privileges, all while trying to persuade Noemi to transfer to his program.

"Aw, come on, Noe," Finn Wilder said as she operated, "What's keeping you in Seattle? We need you."

Noemi had laughed his request off, but she knew he meant it. She was one of the rising stars of cardio on the West Coast—and she'd worked damned hard to get there.

"Finn... one day, maybe."

Finn had been a few years ahead of her, but they'd always had a flirtatious relationship, even in med school. Finn was a cute, dark-blonde boy from Texas with an 'Aww Dad' charm about him. Sexy, too, but Noemi was aware that he was a player and had put him squarely in the Friend Zone, although she did occasionally wonder what a fling with Finn would be like. Fun, hot—and uncomplicated, she guessed.

He gave her his cell number as she left the hospital. "Just in case you feel like some fun," he grinned, utterly confident in his charm. Noemi laughed.

"I'll think about it, Wilder."

SHE WAS STILL LAUGHING as she pulled out onto the Interstate. She had to admit, it felt good to be flirted with. It had been a couple of years since she last dated anyone—even longer since she'd actually slept with anyone.

Noemi went through a mental inventory of what she would have to do when she got to the hospital. She knew Thomasina would have been informed and was probably already in theater, ready for Noemi to arrive. Thank God, Tomi...

She never saw the SUV that was trying to overtake her. All Noemi felt was the shuddering, world-changing shock of being hit—and rolling, rolling, rolling—her scream, her first thought for the precious organ in the plastic cooler beside her, the crippling pain, the smell of gasoline, and her own blood, not dripping, but pouring from her head and then...

...NOTHING.

3

CHAPTER THREE

H er throat was tinder dry. That was the first thing Noemi registered as she crept back up into consciousness. She opened her eyes and saw a window. Bright sunlight. Too bright for winter. She closed her eyes again, smacking her dry lips together.

"Here you are, honey. Ice chip." Something small and cold was slipped into her mouth, and she sucked at it gratefully. Somebody took her hand.

"Sweetheart? Noe?"

Her adoptive mom's voice. "Mom?"

"We're here, darling. Try not to move too much... your father has just gone to fetch Lazlo."

Lazlo. That name meant something, and yet another name was in the front of her mind.

"Thomasina... is she okay? Did she get the heart?" Her voice was so rough—could they hear her?

No one said anything. No, she wasn't making sense. She struggled to sort out what had happened: Car. Heart. Pain.

She blinked some tears away, then felt someone dab at her face. "Momma?" She hadn't called Marian that for years.

"Baby, I'm here. Lazlo is coming... Oh sweetheart."

Noemi could hear her mother's muffled sobs. "I'm okay, Momma."

But she knew she wasn't. There was a commotion, and then Lazlo's kind face moved into view.

"Hey, kiddo, decided to rejoin us?" A bright light was shone in her eyes, and she winced.

"What happened, Laz?"

"You were in a car wreck, kiddo. Drunk driver in an SUV blind-sided you."

"Have you done a CT?"

Lazlo half-smiled. "We've done every test, Noe, the full gamut." He was feeling her neck, and she now heard the bleep-bleep of the machinery.

"I didn't have to have surgery. Good. Was it just cuts and bruises?" Her mouth felt like cotton wool. Lazlo glanced across her at her mother.

He cleared his throat. "Noemi... no. It wasn't just cuts and bruises." He took her hand. "Kiddo, you were seriously injured—a traumatic brain injury. We had to operate to relieve the pressure in your skull, and you suffered three serious strokes. You lost nearly half of your blood volume."

He paused, and Noemi tried to understand what he was telling her. "I'm... How long?"

Lazlo drew in a deep breath. "Five months, Noe. You've been in a coma for five months."

SLOWLY NOEMI DIGESTED ALL the information they were telling her. Five months. Five months since that accident. Her long dark hair was gone, shaved off completely, but she didn't care about that. When Lazlo told her the worst of it, she knew she would have much, much bigger battles to fight.

They had no idea whether she could walk, and certainly she didn't know if she would ever be able to perform surgery again. Her hands, although she could move all of her fingers, shook when she held them up, and her legs felt numb.

"Thomasina..." She had asked again but, in her heart, she had known.

Thomasina was dead. The heart that Noemi had harvested had been destroyed in the accident. "She simply ran out of time," Lazlo told Noemi gently, but it didn't help.

Noemi sobbed for her patient, her charge, her friend, and for Tomi's loved ones. For Rafa and Bepi. Marian held her daughter, as did her father Frank and her sister Leonora, but none of them could comfort her. The guilt was overwhelming.

Dieter came to see her, and his usual arrogance was gone. "Oh, Noe... we nearly lost you." He held her hand and kissed it, but Noemi couldn't feel anything other than pain and loss.

There was some minor brain damage, Lazlo told her, but it would be up to Noemi to gauge the severity. The therapist led her through some simple exercises, but Noemi only grew depressed and irritated as she struggled to make sense of everyday words and phrases.

DURING ONE PARTICULAR SESSION, she sat morosely as the therapist took her through some new exercises. He kept prompting her until Noemi exploded, "For the love of God! I'm not a child!" She then angrily recited an entire surgical procedure to him.

Jeff, the therapist, listened patiently to it all. "Impressive. Now I know how to transplant a heart, but can you tell me what day comes after Thursday—and do it while not being a jackass?"

Noemi stared at him for a long moment, then burst out laughing. Jeff grinned. "That's more like it. Now, I know this can seem like the worst kind of patronizing crap, but what I'm looking for isn't the actual answer—it's your reaction time."

Noemi sighed. "I know. I'm sorry, Jeff. I'm just frustrated."

"I know, but frustration is good. It means you're trying."

Noemi studied him. "Tell me the truth, Jeff. Do you think I'm compos mentis?"

"I absolutely do. It's like anything, Noe. You were shut down for five months, and you have some catching up to do. Practice and you'll get there."

AFTER THAT, Noemi stopped complaining about her rehab and worked harder. She had been relieved that despite the numbness, she could still walk—if a little shakily—and that the tremor in her hands had disappeared as she got stronger.

But she was obsessed with Thomasina's death. When Leonora brought Noemi's laptop from home, Noemi pored over every society page report of Thomasina's funeral. She gazed at the photographs of Rafael Genova, his handsome face masked with pain, holding his son tightly. Dark shadows under his eyes, a half-grown beard... he was so beautiful, even in such terrible grief, that it seemed even more unfair. Noemi touched his face.

"Oh, God, I'm so sorry."

She had asked Lazlo if she could contact Rafa, but he had dissuaded her. "I don't think it would be healthy for either of you."

"I have to apologize."

"Apologize for what? You did nothing wrong, Noe. You got into a wreck with a drunk driver." Lazlo, mild-mannered, sounded angrier than she'd ever heard him. Noemi knew that her colleagues had been forced to save the life of the man who hit her, and that it still rankled.

But that was the oath they had all taken.

Noemi felt useless. She gazed for hours at the photographs of Rafa and Bepi and knew there was nothing she could do to make this right. She read that Rafa took Bepi and moved to San Francisco and had set up a foundation in Thomasina's name.

While Noemi was in a coma, her parents sued the drunk driver who, it turned out, was a wealthy banker from New York. The man settled out of court with them, and Noemi was left with almost a million dollars.

She gave it all to one of Thomasina's foundations. As far as Noemi was concerned it was blood money. Her parents and sister tried to persuade her to keep it, and she offered to give it to them first—but in the end, they gave her their blessing. "It's yours to do with what you want," Frank Castor said, his hand on his daughter's shoulder.

Noemi didn't hesitate. A month later, they allowed her to go home —to her parent's house. Two weeks later, Noemi insisted on going home to her own apartment. Lazlo wouldn't let her come back to work yet. "You need to heal."

NOEMI STARED at her reflection in the mirror of her bathroom. The apartment—her haven, her comfort for so long—rang with loneliness. In the mirror was a woman she didn't recognize. Only her eyes, large, dark brown, and sad, seemed the same. Her dark hair had begun to grow out, but it would be months before it felt like her hair again. Her skin, usually such a rich caramel color, was yellow and wan.

Noemi closed her eyes and sighed. The depression was beginning to drag her down, make her lose all hope of returning to her former life, and she desperately needed to do something to make herself feel human again. A vacation? No. She wouldn't be able to enjoy it knowing that Thomasina was in her grave, her family shattered. Noemi kept seeing Rafa's face as he stood at his dead fiancée's funeral.

It wasn't until after she had been in rehab for a few months that Noemi suddenly realized what she had to do. While attending a group session with a bunch of people recovering from various injuries, she had started talking to a young woman recently returned from a tour in Afghanistan.

"We needed doctors," she told Noemi. "Everything was in such poor supply: drugs, docs, basic supplies."

It was then Noemi had the idea. Médecins Sans Frontières. Doctors Without Borders. Noemi went to Lazlo first who encouraged her to complete her rehab first.

"You'll need to be at your peak condition for that," he warned, "but I understand why you want to go. Your job is safe, Noe. Just promise you'll come back to us."

Her family were less understanding. "Stop beating yourself up for something that wasn't your fault." Leonora said, her face creased with worry.

Noemi hugged her four-year-old nephew Jack close. The child wriggled in her arms wanting to get off of her lap, but Noemi needed to hug him. "I know it wasn't... but something in me needs to do something to redress the balance."

"You and that damn karma." Leo was pissed off, and Noemi felt badly for her sister, knowing it was because she was worried.

"Leo... please. I need at least one of you to be on my side." Noemi's voice cracked, and Leo's face softened.

"Oh, sweetie..."

THEY DECIDED NOT to tell their parents until everything was settled, but to their surprise, Marian and Frank were stoic. "We knew something was coming," Marian told her daughters, "so this isn't unexpected. Do what you need to do, Noe. Just please stay safe."

"I will."

THE DAY before she flew to Syria, Noemi asked her family to give her some time alone. She took a cab out to the cemetery where Thomasina Ballentine was buried and laid flowers on the other woman's grave. "I'm so sorry, Tomi. You deserved better."

She stayed there for a time before turning to go. She looked up and froze. Rafael Genova was standing a little way behind her, watching her with an unreadable expression on his face. Noemi didn't know what to say to him. The pain in his eyes was unbearable to see.

"Rafa... Mr. Genova... words can't express how sorry I am..."

Rafa turned and walked away from her, stumbling a little. Noemi felt tears drop down her cheeks. "Oh, Rafa," she whispered, "I'm so sorry..."

THE NEXT MORNING, she got on a plane and flew to the Middle East, not knowing whether she would ever come back.

4

CHAPTER FOUR

T wo years later...

NOEMI SHRUGGED into her white coat and shut her locker. There was no good reason why she should be so nervous—after all, this was her home, her hospital. But on this, her first day back at the Seattle workplace she'd known so well, she felt like a stranger.

"Hey, kiddo! Come walk with me, would you?" Lazlo smiled at her as he appeared at the door of the changing room.

Noemi smiled and nodded, joining her old friend and mentor as they walked through the hospital. Lazlo smiled at her.

"Now... there's something I didn't tell you when you first came back, and I've struggled with how to share it with you."

"Lazlo, I told you—I don't care that Finn is my superior now. I haven't been doing much cardio surgery and I'm behind. We both knew that if I went to Syria, my training would suffer, and I'd have to catch up—and I have new skills now that we might find useful."

"It's not that." Lazlo stopped and fixed her with a steady gaze. "Rafael Genova is now on the Board of the hospital."

That she wasn't expecting. "I thought he moved away."

"He did, but he came back. He told me he couldn't be away from Thomasina, and that Bepi wanted to visit his momma's resting place. Rafa told me if he couldn't escape the pain, he wanted to at least face it head on and to do something positive. I thought you should know, Noemi."

She nodded, her emotions in turmoil. Noemi had counted on the fact that she wouldn't run into Rafa again, that he was safely in San Francisco, or she might not have agreed to come back to Seattle. Don't be a coward. "It's fine, Lazlo. It's not like I run in the same circles as the Board."

Lazlo nodded but Noemi sensed he wasn't done. "And then there's the clinic."

"The clinic?"

"The Thomasina Ballentine Clinic for Cardiology."

It was a shock to her entire being. "What?"

"And Rafa wants you to run it."

Noemi couldn't breathe. "What?" Lazlo must have been aware of this way before she returned home—was she being punished? "Lazlo... I...I can't."

"Yes, you can. Now, obviously, until you're an attending, you'll be supervised, but yes, I and the Board agreed—you are the person to lead this."

From his voice, Noemi could tell that her friend was nervous about pulling rank on her like this. "Are you trying to punish me?"

"Far from it, Noe. You've had two years, and the moment you came back from Syria, I could tell you still hadn't forgiven yourself for Thomasina. You still haven't processed it."

"You don't know what I saw in Syria, Lazlo."

"I can guess, and no doubt you're blaming yourself for not saving more people. That is your Achilles' heel, Noe. You are not God. You can't save everyone. Until you learn that, you'll never be the exemplary doctor I know you can be."

Noemi stopped walking. It was a lot to process all at once. Lazlo's expression softened. "Noemi... I would not be pushing you like this unless I believed in you. I believe in you. The hospital believes in you. Rafael Genova is not punishing you for Thomasina's death. He's offering you the chance to honor her. Take it."

And Noemi had no idea how to say no.

SHE WALKED into the new clinic, breathing in the smells of fresh paint and of new equipment barely out of its plastic. It wasn't open yet, Lazlo had told her—a ceremony was planned for two days' time, and Noemi knew that Rafa, Bepi, and Thomasina's family would be there. Thomasina's name was above the doorway, her photograph and biography framed at reception.

Noemi read it through and half-smiled at the photograph. It was Thomasina laughing, radiant, and full of joie de vivre, and Noemi realized that she had missed the sight of her patient—her friend.

"Hey, girl," she murmured, touching the photograph.

"Getting emotional?"

Noemi turned with a smile. Finn Wilder grinned back at her. "Welcome back, honey." He gave her a hug, then rubbed her back. "How're the legs?"

"Good. A two-year tour at the run-down hospital facilities in Syria will do that. Exercise was mandatory. So," she added, narrowing her eyes at him, "Lazlo finally managed to poach you from Tacoma?"

"What can I say? I'm a sucker for a pretty face."

Noemi laughed. "Well, it's going to be good to work for you, Finn."

"With me, Noe. With. Anything else is just ego—we'll make a great team."

Noemi shook her head. "You're so different from what I'm used to."

Finn laughed. "You mean Dr. Dieter WonderDick?"

"The very one." Noemi suddenly felt disloyal. "Although, he was great to me, when... you know."

"You know that wasn't your fault."

"Why does everyone keep saying that to me?"

"Because, Noe, you carry this... Aw, hell, don't worry about it. I'm sure you've heard all this before." Finn sighed, knowing he'd opened a wound. "Let me show you around. Look at all the nice new toys we have. Genova gave us a huge amount, you know."

"I figured."

Finn showed her all the new equipment. "And we've funds for research too."

"Really?"

"Really. The guy gave us a billion."

Noemi stopped. "What?"

"Yep."

Noemi was stunned. "He gave a billion dollars to the hospital where his fiancée died?"

"No," Finn half-smiled at her. "He gave a billion dollars to the doctor he believes in, and who blames herself for Thomasina's death. He gave a billion dollars to you, Noe. To your future."

NOEMI'S EMOTIONS were in turmoil. Why would Rafa do this? Despite what Finn said, Noemi couldn't believe Rafa's motives were that pure.

Later, at home, she mindlessly ate some cold pizza and took a long bath. Had it been a mistake to come back? Everyone seemed to be determined to make her face what had happened—hadn't she been through enough?

She went to bed but couldn't sleep. Time ticked by, and at one a.m., having thought herself into a panic, she got up and threw her jeans on over her underwear, shrugging into a sweatshirt.

She was on the road before she could talk herself out of it. Rafael's mansion was well-known, nestling as it did along the shores of Lake Washington. Noemi didn't know if she would be able to get past the gate, but she needed to try. She needed to see him, to ask him if he was just interested in torturing her. She knew she was overtired and stressed, but she didn't care.

To her surprise, the guard at the gate waved her through. "Mr. Genova has been expecting you, Dr. Castor."

His words merely fueled the anger that was building up inside her. She parked her car in front of the house and stormed up the steps. The door was open and she went in, but her courage abandoned her when she saw him.

"Hi, Noemi."

Rafael Genova was waiting for her.

5

_____

CHAPTER FIVE

The sight of him made her stop and think about what she was doing. Noemi passed a hand over her eyes, her adrenaline deserting her. "I don't know why I'm here."

Rafa came to her and offered her his hand. "To talk. If you don't mind, can we go to the other side of the house? Bepi is sleeping and if you need to scream..."

Noemi didn't feel like screaming, but she let him lead her into another room. The room was obviously a study, his den, filled with bookshelves and battered old couches, it belied the opulence of the rest of the mansion.

She turned to study Rafa. He had aged since she had last seen him, his handsome face now seemingly always masked in sadness, his green eyes ringed with dark lashes were wary and exhausted. Noemi knew instantly that Rafa wasn't trying to take his revenge on her or the hospital; he was merely trying to find meaning in Thomasina's death.

Rafa made her some hot tea. She thanked him and took the cup. "They said you were expecting me."

He sat down opposite her, nodding. "I was. I have been. Actually, I expected you to come at me as soon as you found out."

"I thought you were tormenting me. Now, I feel stupid—and ashamed."

"Don't. The whole reason I'm doing this is so that you will stop blaming yourself. Tomi would have hated it. The accident wasn't your fault; Tomi's illness wasn't either. It's just dumb bad luck." He sighed, rubbing his eyes. "I wanted to see you. That day at Tomi's grave... I should have told you then that I didn't blame you. I called Lazlo the next day, but he told me where you'd gone. I should have... God, I don't know, Noemi. I'm still trying to figure all of this out."

"How is Bepi?"

Rafa smiled then and his face lit up. "My joy. He's so resilient, you know? I wish we didn't lose that as we got older. Got old. I got old."

Noemi wanted to touch his face. "You're not old."

"I feel old. After Tomi died, I had to focus on Bepi, getting him through the grief..."

"... and who helped you get through the grief, Rafa?"

He didn't answer. "Bepi is the priority."

Noemi, calm now, drew in a deep breath. "Rafa, what is it you want the clinic to achieve? I mean, we can treat cardio patients, research new methods and new protocols, but none of it will bring Tomi back. Why? Why is it your job to fund this?"

"Because no one else is able to, at least not to the extent that I am. Look, I know nothing—nothing about medicine. What I know is shipping—as dull as that sounds. What I do have is money, and if I keep it all.... why? What else could I possibly want? As long as my son is happy, healthy, and secure?" His shoulders slumped. "Noemi... No. It won't bring Tomi back. But it might prevent the kind of pain that —" He trailed off and let out a shaky breath.

Noemi felt her heart go out to him. "I just don't know if I'm the right person to lead it. I'm just a resident, Rafa."

"I just want you involved. Tomi loved you. She trusted you, and her death doesn't change that."

"Do you trust me, Rafa?" The question came to her, and she already knew the answer. He smiled sadly.

"I'm trying. But know this—I do not blame you in any way for

Thomasina's death. Perhaps, between us, we can make it so it wasn't such a damn waste." Rafa looked at Noemi with those startling green eyes and something deep inside her awoke. Hope. Reason. That's what it is, she told herself, nothing more.

"I can't promise we'll make any progress."

"Let's just try. What do you say?"

And looking deep into his eyes, Noemi knew she couldn't say no.

SHE FOUND, over the next few weeks, that Rafa was a regular visitor to the clinic, always interested in what they were doing but never making them feel like he was questioning their methods. He took a genuine interest in the medicine and spent time talking to everyone about what they needed to make progress.

He would often arrive as she was finishing her shift and ask her to join him for coffee. "If you're not too tired," he would add. "Or if you have other plans."

The truth was Noemi looked forward to seeing him. Sometimes he would bring Bepi with him, and the boy would entertain them both.

As Noemi regained her confidence, she found working with Finn Wilder was inspiring. Unlike Dieter, whom she'd worked with before the accident, Finn had no interest in power mongering—he wanted to help Noemi reach her full potential.

Noemi threw herself back into work, and to all outward appearances, she appeared confident and together. It was only when she was alone at night that the nightmares came—and now, they weren't only about Thomasina.

Noemi had yet to deal with what she'd experienced while working in Syria: the terrible hardships, the horrific things she had seen. Without thinking of the repercussions, she had often thrown herself into the most dangerous situations, frequently working under fire to help save the civilians trapped between warring factions.

It had been the children, the orphans, who had affected her most: their confusion about why this was happening, why grown men were killing each other, their mothers, and their friends... they had haunted Noemi. She'd made some good friends out there but making friends was dangerous—on more than one occasion, she had lost someone. They had all lost people.

She had to make herself numb to get through each day, and now that she was back in Seattle safe, she was surprised to find herself getting angry at the smallest things: the way people walked blithely down the street, not having to watch out for sniper fire or rogue bombs. Did they appreciate it? Noemi would stomp into work in a foul mood which she then had to struggle to control. Irrational mood swings plagued her now, but she kept them hidden, often disappearing into the stalls of the restrooms to practice deep breathing.

Noemi told herself it would pass; she was just readjusting to being back in the States. But the only time she ever really found peace was when she was with Rafael Genova—and she didn't want to even consider the reason for that.

Rafael Genova picked his son up from his kindergarten, ignoring the admiring glances of the mommies present. He knew the effect his good looks had on women, but his shattered heart was only now healing itself, and he couldn't even think of another woman yet.

Except...

He told himself that the reason why he was spending so much time with Noemi Castor was his investment in the hospital and the clinic. When Thomasina had been alive, his entire world had been her and Bepi, but even then, he had been drawn to the young doctor —although he would have never ever cheated on Thomasina.

Noemi Castor reminded him of a time in his life when he too had been able to follow his passion: before his elder brother, Zani, had decided he wanted no part of their father's shipping business and had taken his trust fund and disappeared to party in Europe—and Rafa had to take up the mantle; a time when he had wanted to go to college to study anything but shipping. There were several educational routes open to him: his 4.0 GPA saw to that. He'd been torn between art and science, but then Zani had let his father down, and Rafa knew he had to step up to the plate.

Twenty years later, he'd guided his father's enterprise up into the stratosphere, but it didn't feed Rafa's soul. He was aware that now he was living vicariously through his involvement with the hospital, and he knew that, selfishly, it was a link forever to Tomi.

Thomasina had been his best friend, his romantic partner, his confidante. They'd met at a party held by one of his mother's society friends. Rafa, ever loyal to his beloved mother, hated social functions, but when he'd seen the beautiful blonde sneaking a cigarette outside and looking as bored as he did, he perked up.

Their friendship had been almost immediate, and their romance came later when they both knew they couldn't live without each other, making each other laugh constantly and not taking their 'positions' in society seriously. Thomasina had survived the whole cotillion set with her mother and elder sister by embracing an irreverence that had landed her in finishing school in Switzerland—from which she got herself expelled, of course.

Thomasina didn't want to be lauded for her physical appearance; she had wanted to use her not inconsiderable intellect. Her mother, heiress to a newspaper fortune, disapproved of Rafa right up to the moment Bepi was born. Thomasina had gotten pregnant by mistake, but they both agreed: Bepi was the best thing that ever happened to them; it brought both families together. But Thomasina fell ill and everything changed.

Rafael took Bepi to his favorite ice cream parlor, a weekly treat he knew Bepi loved. Thomasina had always taken him, and so Rafa continued that tradition. Today though, he noticed his son was quieter than normal.

"What is it, slugger?"

Bepi shook his head, not meeting his father's gaze. He swirled the ice cream around in his bowl but didn't eat any. Finally, Rafa pushed the dishes away.

"Come on, sport. Talk to Pa."

Bepi wriggled, obviously uncomfortable. "Pa... why did Momma have to go away?"

Rafa's heart hurt. "We talked about this, kiddo. Momma was sick, and although she tried to get better, she couldn't. You know what it means when someone dies, right? They leave their body and go to sleep forever." He stroked his son's hair back. "Why do you ask today?"

"Mikey's daddy is getting a new mommy for him."

Ah. Rafa hoisted his son onto his lap. "Well, maybe one day, I might meet a lady who will want to be your... well, not your Momma, but someone who will want to love you like Momma did."

Bepi nodded, but Rafa could see the tears in his son's eyes. "Hey, buddy, we're doing okay, right? You and me?" An idea came to him. "Listen... remember we talked about getting a dog? From the shelter?"

Bepi immediately brightened. "We can go?"

"Sure we can."

"Tonight?"

Rafa laughed. Oh, what the hell... "If you've finished your dessert, we can go right now."

Bepi was off his lap before Rafa finished his sentence.

6
___

CHAPTER SIX

Noemi had been thinking about it since returning from Syria, and now she was absolutely sure it was the right decision. She crouched down at the door of the cage and offered her hand to the dog. The huge German Shepard, all fluff, sniffed her hand gingerly and then slunk out of the cage to her. Noemi wrapped her arms around the dog. "Hello, buddy."

The dog licked her face and Noemi giggled. She smiled up at the shelter assistant. "She's definitely the one."

The assistant smiled. "Well, I'm very happy for you both. She's an absolute sweetheart, but most people want a younger dog. Mouse here needs a loving home, and the good thing is she's house-trained."

"I live close enough to the hospital that I can go back and forth so she doesn't get fussy." Noemi was beyond excited. When she'd come to the shelter a few days ago, she'd fallen for Mouse immediately—not least because of the incongruous name. Mouse was huge! Leonora had expressed doubts whether Noemi's five-five frame could handle such a big dog. Noemi had no such qualms. The shelter had let her take Mouse for a few walks on her nightly visits, and she knew she could handle her new roommate just fine.

Noemi signed all the paperwork she needed to and made a large donation to the shelter. She was just walking out with Mouse when she saw Rafael Genova and Bepi walking towards her. Bepi exclaimed and ran to her. Noemi hugged the little boy. "Hey, cutie pie."

Bepi hugged her back then turned his attention to Mouse, his eyes wide. "It's okay, Bepi," Noemi said gently, "This is Mouse. She likes to be petted."

Bepi put out an uncertain hand, and Mouse licked it. Bepi grinned and began to stroke the dog's thick fur. Mouse rested her face against Bepi's, and Noemi's heart thumped. Dogs were a joy. Just utter joy and love.

She looked up and smiled at Rafa. "I didn't expect to see you here."

"I've been promising Bepi a dog for a while... although I think he's already fallen for your delightful mutt."

Noemi laughed. "Sorry, Bepi. But there are more puppies inside all needing a home. I bet you'll find one just as lovely as Mouse."

"Will you come and help us look, Nommy?" Bepi was clearly not ready to let Mouse out of his sight just yet.

"Noe might want to go home, Bepi," his father said gently but Noemi smiled.

"No, I don't mind. It'll be fun... if you don't mind?" She met Rafa's gaze and something undefinable passed between them.

"No," he said, softly. "I don't mind at all."

Noemi felt her face burn and looked away from Rafa. She held her free hand out to Bepi. "Come on then. Let's go find you a puppy."

RAFA TUCKED Bepi into his bed. It was past ten o'clock already, but the overexcited little boy wouldn't settle as he talked nonstop to Rafa and Noemi. He had insisted that Noemi and Mouse come back to the house—Rafa suspected so that he could play with Mouse—and now, finally, Bepi had fallen asleep.

Rafa went back down to the living room. Mouse was stretched out on the rug, fast asleep, and Noemi sat by her dog, running her hands through the dog's plush fur.

Lucky dog...

Rafa smiled at her. "She is a beautiful mutt."

"Isn't she? I'm so delighted with her." Noemi smiled at him shyly. "I must go. I've stayed far too long as it is, but Bepi is such an adorable kid."

"Thank you. I think so, but please, stay a little while longer. It's nice to have some adult conversation for once."

Noemi chuckled but nodded. "Okay, I'd like that."

Rafa sat down on the floor next to them. Mouse woke and sleepily shifted her head, so it rested on his knee.

"She likes you. That's always a good character assessment."

Rafa smiled at Noemi. Her hair, now grown even longer than before the accident, fell in soft waves past her shoulders. Her lovely face, with sweetly plump cheeks and shining brown eyes, was younger than her thirty-years-old. Without thinking, Rafa reached out and stroked her cheek.

Noemi froze and jerked away, and Rafa dropped his hand. "God, I'm sorry... I don't know what came over me."

Noemi's face was bright red, and she scrambled to her feet. "I think I'd better go."

"Maybe that is for the best."

Noemi woke her dog gently. "Come on, Mouse."

He walked her to her car. "Look, I'm sorry. That was completely inappropriate, Noemi, and I'd hate to think a moment's thoughtless-ness ruined our... friendship."

"It's okay, Rafa, really. I'll see you around."

Rafa watched her drive away, remonstrating with himself. What the hell happened? On the face of it—no pun intended—I just touched her face. But it was the intimacy of the moment that had shocked them both... no way were they good enough, close enough friends for that.

"Oh, God damn it." Rafa pinched the bridge of his nose. He stayed outside for a few minutes, breathing in the cold night air.

What with Bepi fretting about Tomi's absence in his life... there was only one thing to do. He had to move on and get Noemi Castor out of his head. There were plenty of women lining up to console the bereaved fiancée—he would ask his assistant to set up a date with one of them. He would not fuck up his life, Bepi's life, and Noemi Castor's life by acting out a crush when it was so wholly inappropriate.

Yes, he thought, going back inside. It's time to move on.

NOEMI STRIPPED out of her clothes and fell onto the bed. Mouse immediately followed her, and Noemi cuddled up to the large dog, pulling the comforter over them both. "You and me now, Mousie."

But her skin burned where Rafa had touched her, and as she relived that moment—that all-too-brief moment—her body felt warm, and a pulse beat frantically between her legs. It had stunned her, the tenderness of it, his beautiful green eyes on hers, but it had been so unexpected that she had pulled away when what she really wanted to do was kiss him. She had never been so attracted to anyone in her life, and for that split second, she would have thrown everything away.

Because she and Rafa together would be a disaster. There was too much water under the bridge—too much guilt, too much shame.

Noemi sighed now. She had to get over this... crush. That's all it is: a crush. What red-blooded woman wouldn't have a crush on Rafael Genova? The man was built like a Roman God, and that face—that gorgeous face with so much sadness etched into it...

"Stop it," she groaned and buried her face in Mouse's fur. The dog grumbled a little, and she chuckled. "Sorry, boo."

But when she fell asleep that night, she dreamed of Rafael's lips against hers, his skin on hers, his hands on her body, and his cock driving her onwards to that ultimate pleasure...

CHAPTER SEVEN

Lazlo called Noemi into his office a week later. "Hey, kiddo, I have some news. As you know, there's a general surgeon gig up for grabs."

Noemi looked alarmed. "Laz, cardio is my..."

He shook his head, grinning. "Not for you. It's just I've been in talks with someone you might know from your time in Doctors Without Borders. Kit Vaughan?"

Noemi smiled. "Of course! Ah man, Kit's coming here? That's great news."

"Well, he's coming to meet me to discuss it at least. I was wondering if you'd help me try to get him to commit?"

"No problem. When's he coming?"

"This morning."

Noemi chuckled, rolling her eyes. "Nothing like a bit of notice, Laz."

"I didn't want to jinx it." Lazlo grinned, unrepentant, and Noemi pretended to scowl at him.

"For scientists, we sure are a superstitious bunch around here. No problem about Kit; just page me when he gets here. I won't let him leave the place without giving you a yes."

Lazlo studied her, and although Noemi was about to leave, she sensed he had more to say. "What's up?"

"You know... it is within my power to make you an attending, Noe. You have the experience."

Noemi was confused. "Finn's the cardio attending and honestly, I'm happy where I am. The clinic is my new baby." She felt her face burn as she mentioned it, thinking of Rafa, but pushed the thought away. "I can treat patients and do research."

"I could make you a Research Attending."

Noemi chewed her lip. "It's not that it's not tempting, Laz, but I won't feel as if I've earned it. What with being out of action for a year, then going abroad... I'd be stepping on some toes. Dieter wouldn't like it."

"Pah, who cares what Dieter thinks?"

"He thinks I'm not ready, and for once, I agree."

Lazlo sat back, sighing. "If you have one fault, Noe, it's your staggering and unwarranted lack of self-confidence. That is the only thing holding you back. You don't have the killer instinct, that arrogance that means the difference between you being the best surgeon I've even nurtured... and, well...you."

Noemi blinked, Lazlo's observations coming out of nowhere. "I'm getting there, Laz."

He nodded. "But not as quickly as you should. Want a nickel's worth of free advice?"

"Always."

"Break the rules. Professionally and privately. Push the boundaries, upset a few people, and then don't apologize for it. I want to see you soar, Noemi Castor. Remember that."

Noemi was still thinking about what Lazlo had told her as she sat in the cafeteria at lunchtime. Ally was moaning to Dieter about his behavior in surgery.

Dieter was shrugging. "Got the result we wanted though, didn't I?"

"You can do it without being a total douche bag, though."

Dieter grinned at her, leaning his chin on her shoulder. Ally pushed him away and Dieter laughed.

He nudged a toe at Noemi's leg. "Hey, Spacecakes. You with us?"

Noemi shook herself. "Sorry. Just thinking about stuff."

"Holy damnation and all that is glorious…" Ally suddenly sat up straight, staring over Noemi's shoulder. "I have died and gone to heaven."

Noemi looked around to see who Ally was lusting after. An extremely tall, surfer-blonde God was stalking towards them, a huge grin on his face. Noemi gave a cry of happiness and leapt up. The God grabbed her and swung her around in a bear hug.

"Noemi-bloody-Castor!"

"Kit, you big lug! Put me down!" She was giggling furiously. Kit beamed at the table, winking at Ally. "Everyone, this is Kit Vaughan, General Surgery God, despot, man whore, slut! Ow, ow!" Noemi giggled as Kit tickled her. He stuck his hand out and shook Ally's hand.

"How you doing? … and you are?" His Australian accent boomed out over the cafeteria, attracting the attention of the other hospital staff, Noemi saw.

"Ally… short for Available," Ally said, and Noemi snorted with laughter.

"Kit, you might have met your match with Ally. This is Dieter."

Dieter and Kit shook hands, sizing each other up. Noemi was relieved when Dieter didn't start a pissing contest; he just nodded to them and moved away.

Ally left them alone—reluctantly—and Noemi showed Kit around the hospital.

"It's my job to persuade you to join us," she grinned at her friend. "And believe me, I'm going to go all out."

"I would expect nothing less after seeing what you did in Syria."

"How is everyone?" It was the question she was dreading asking and yet the one she needed to know. Kit met her gaze.

"Everyone's... alive. But sometimes, alive doesn't mean everything is rosy, you know?"

"It's bad?"

Kit nodded. "I think you got out when you should have. Some of the guys, Rick, Flynn, Sarah... they're shattered, Noe. But we have to keep fighting to help people."

"I know. It's been on my mind to go back, but before I do, I need to build a life for myself here."

Kit smiled. "How's it been? I hear you got yourself a sugar daddy."

Noemi winced, and Kit put his hand on her shoulder. "Hey, I'm kidding. I meant the clinic. Lazlo wouldn't shut up about it."

Noemi chuckled. "Let me show you around. Believe me, I'll be needing some of your skills if I'm going to make a success of it."

They walked to the Thomasina Ballentine Clinic, and Kit stopped outside the front door, looking up at the signage. "You know, I used to know her stepbrother, Drew. He's something in the church... I don't know."

"I never met him. I met her fiancée, of course. They have the cutest little boy."

"Feeling broody, kid?" Kit grinned at her as always, flirting. Noemi laughed.

"If the next line out of your mouth is about having my eggs fertilized..."

"Gah, as if I'd be that unoriginal." He hooked an arm around her shoulders. "But now that you mention it..."

She pushed him away, laughing. "Dude, this isn't Grey's Anatomy."

Kit made a face. "What, no shagging in the on-call room?"

"None." She made a disapproving face. "So unhygienic."

"Says the girl who watches Dr. Mike's YouTube channel religiously, but never with anyone else present."

Noemi giggled. "You have a filthy mind, Vaughan. Now, act doctorly, and come with me."

· · ·

KIT'S ARRIVAL seemed to give everyone a boost. He signed a three-year contract with a delighted Lazlo, and Noemi helped him find an apartment in the city. He also made friends with Mouse, and Noemi would take Mouse over to his neighborhood to walk before her shifts.

Within a couple of weeks, Kit had made himself at home. Despite his flirtatious manner, he was an exemplary surgeon, and Noemi loved to watch him operate.

Dieter's nose was only slightly out of joint. Even he could see Kit's presence had lifted the morale of the staff. Still, he renewed his advances to Noemi, who very gently let him down. "Is it because of the blonde Australian?" Dieter asked her when she'd turned down his third invitation to dinner.

No, it's because of the dark Italian...

Noemi couldn't get Rafael out of her head. They hadn't seen each other since that night, but every time she looked at Mouse, she remembered her dog's head resting so peacefully on Rafa's knee, how natural it seemed for them to be sitting together on his rug, spending time together. God, she dreamed about his lips on hers...

"For the love of God, stop it." She cussed softly as she sat in the ladies' restroom, then jumped when she heard Ally's voice.

"You talking to yourself again, hon?"

Noemi exited the stall and washed her hands as she heard the other toilet flush. Ally grinned at her as she joined her at the sink. "You okay?"

Noemi hesitated, then checked they were alone. "Hypothetical."

"Okay."

"There's someone I've been... He's... a friend. Sort of."

"Before you go on, if you've fucked Kit Vaughan..." Ally said warningly.

"Not Kit, he's all yours," Noemi laughed. "No, this is someone... not at the hospital. Kind of. He's a friend of a patient, let's say. We're sort of friends. But, I can't stop thinking about him."

"Then fuck him, if that's what you want." Ally shrugged, and Noemi wishes she too could be twenty-five and as confident as Ally.

"But it would ruin our friendship."

"Are you really that good friends with him?"

Again, Noemi hesitated, and Ally made a face. "See? Jeez, Noe, when was the last time you got laid?"

"Three..."

"Months? Fuck, get on it."

"... years," Noemi finished. "Not since before the accident." Not since before Thomasina died.

Ally was flabbergasted. "Years? Three years, Noe? How is that possible?" She grabbed Noemi's arm and made her look in the mirror. "Look at you. You look like a freaking supermodel, you have curves to die for, I want your boobs, and every man in this place would kill to fuck you. Jesus, Noe, after everything you've been through, live."

Ally seemed to realize she sounded angry and smiled ruefully. "Sorry, but you've been on a deathwatch for years now. You're thirty years old and gorgeous. Go for him, whoever he is. Leap."

She patted Noemi's shoulder and left her alone. Noemi stared at her reflection. Ally was right. Work was her passion, but she needed something else too.

When Ally invited her to the bar with Kit, Dieter, and some other people that night, Noemi agreed. "I have to go home first to walk Mouse, but I promise, I'll join you later."

WHEN SHE GOT HOME, Mouse greeted her with wild abandon, and Noemi hugged her dog to her. "Gonna get a life, baby," she murmured. She walked the dog for an hour, then went home to shower.

Deciding what to wear, she chose a simple spaghetti-strapped mini dress, showing off her long legs for once, light makeup, and a simple gold chain which hung between her breasts. She left her dark hair down, clouding around her.

. . .

Kit whistled, and Ally beamed at her as she made her way into the bar. "Damn, girl."

Noemi flushed pink and distracted them from all the compliments by asking what they were drinking. An hour later, a beer down, and she started to relax, enjoying the company of her friends. She and Ally chatted, then watched in amusement as Dieter tried to play power games with Kit at the pool table. Good-naturedly, Kit conceded every point to Dieter, and Noemi watched as Dieter gave up his games, and instead began enjoying the company of the other man.

"So, you never really did that?" Ally nodded at Kit, and Noemi chuckled.

"I really never did. I wasn't exactly in the right headspace when I got over there, and believe me, sex was the last thing on everybody's minds."

"Understandable. But what about now?"

Noemi smiled at her friend. "I told you. You want to go for it, do it. Kit and I are firmly in the Friend Zone. Almost like siblings now."

"Eww, sexy sibs. Like Angelina and James Haven."

Noemi looked blank, and Ally rolled her eyes. "God, watch Bravo now and again. Or read The Enquirer. One or the other."

Noemi was amused. "Any other tips for this old lady?"

"Yeah. You look a million dollars. Try to find someone in here to hook up with, would you?"

"Baby steps, Al. Now, look. Kit's on his own. Why don't you go work your magic?"

Dieter was at the bar, chatting to a pretty blonde woman, and Noemi took some time to check out the rest of the bar. Too many hospital folks here for any random under-the-wire hookups, and Noemi felt out of practice. When Dieter came back to the table, she excused herself and went to the restrooms. She splashed water on her face, feeling the effects of the beer. She was such a lightweight when it came to alcohol. She shook her head, smiling.

Going back out, she walked along the dark corridor that led back to the bar. The men's restroom door opened towards her and she froze.

Rafael Genova stopped, blinked. They stared at each other for a long moment...

... and then his lips were on hers.

CHAPTER EIGHT

N oemi barely had time to take a breath before they kissed, but she didn't care. It was everything she had dreamed of: soft, then rough as they both moaned with pent-up desire. Rafael picked her up, and she wrapped her legs around his waist as he pushed out of the side-door and into the back alley of the bar.

Noemi's fingers were tangled in his hair, and she had no idea where he was taking her, but she didn't care. She could not get enough of his mouth on hers, his fresh, clean cologne flooding her senses.

Then, in a flash, they were in his Mercedes and driving through Seattle's streets. Neither of them said a word, but their fingers linked. Rafa drove to Noemi's apartment and, hand-in-hand, they walked up the stairs together.

He followed her in, slipping his hand onto her waist. "Are you sure?" He said at last and she nodded.

His lips were against hers again then, and she sunk into the kiss. With his broad build and height, she felt tiny in his embrace, and when he swept her up into his arms, Noemi found she couldn't look away from his gaze. Oh, how I want you...

She nodded along the hallway to her bedroom and Rafa walked

quickly. In the bedroom, he set her down on her feet, and they embraced again, tenderly this time. Noemi's fingers, trembling, moved to the buttons of his shirt. She pressed her lips against the skin of his chest, then laid her head against it. She could feel the quick, hammering beat of his heart and she sighed. Her own heart was banging hard against her chest.

Rafa tilted her chin up with a finger and kissed her. "You don't know how long I've waited for this," he murmured, and a thrill ran through her.

"Rafa..."

"Shh..." He kissed her again and then he was sliding the spaghetti straps of her dress down her shoulders, and the dress fell to the floor.

Rafa sucked in a deep breath. "Christ, you're exquisite."

He swept her onto the bed, quickly stripping down to his underwear and covering her body with his. Noemi kissed him hungrily, not wanting to miss a moment of this. She reached down to cup his cock through his underwear, feeling the hot length of it stiffen as she stroked it. Rafa groaned and buried his face in her neck, his lips against her throat. "Noemi..."

She hooked her legs around him, sliding her hands into his dark curls. She made him look up at her. "I want you so much, Rafa. Fuck me, please, just... fuck me."

He gathered her to him as each explored the other's body, skin against skin, their gazes locked. Rafa slid her panties down her thighs, moving down her body, his lips trailing down her belly until they found her sex.

Noemi shivered with pleasure as his tongue lashed around her clit. He expertly teased her until it became so unbearably sensitive that the merest flick of his tongue sent powerful waves of ecstasy through her body. Her skin felt like it was on fire, and she begged him to be inside her.

Rafa snagged a condom from his jeans. "Help me with this, would you, my darling?"

My darling... Noemi felt giddy like a teenager, and her fingers were trembling as she rolled the rubber down his huge, thick cock.

Rafa smiled down at her as he pushed inside her, and Noemi moaned at the sweet sensation of him filling her.

They moved together, finding their rhythm easily. Rafa's lips were rough against hers, his need for her seemingly animal and feral. He murmured her name over and over as they made love, and when Noemi felt her climax explode through her body, she gasped, giving a long moan of release. "Oh, Rafa... Rafa..."

His body shuddered with his own orgasm, his green eyes intense as he came, and then as they recovered all-entangled, he smiled down at her. "Hey, beautiful."

Noemi, much to her eternal embarrassment, burst into tears.

RAFA HELD her as she sobbed, his lips pressed against her temple. He wasn't fazed by her tears—it was just as emotional for him. He hadn't slept with anyone since Thomasina and now, with this beautiful woman in his arms, he knew he had been right to wait. He hadn't been able to stop thinking about Noemi since that day by Thomasina's grave. Noemi, so injured, her lovely face etched with guilt and grief... he'd wanted to comfort her, but at Tomi's grave, and with the wound so raw, he had turned away from her.

Now, he waited until she had cried herself out. "Okay?"

She nodded. "Sorry, I'm so sorry, I don't know what came over me."

"It's okay, baby. This has been... intense."

She gave a choked laugh. "You can say that again." She looked up at him, her dark eyes huge. "I'm still not sure it actually happened."

Rafa laughed. "Trust me... it did."

She stroked his face. "I can't stop thinking about you. I wish I could; it just doesn't seem right. Thomasina..."

"... is gone. There's nothing for us to feel guilty about. She adored you, Noe. I adore you." He kissed her. "Look, I loved Tomi with all my heart. Nothing will ever change that. But who says you only get one chance of love in a lifetime?" He sat up, running a hand through his hair. "For a long time, I tried to deny that what I felt for you was anything but a crush. I'm forty years old but when I'm near you, I feel like a teenage boy."

Noemi curled her body against his, and he wrapped his arms around her. "Rafa... my head is a mess. I just don't know if I'm good enough for you."

"Don't ever say that."

"I mean it. My head is a nightmare. The accident. Tomi. What I saw in Syria. We have to think about Bepi, what's good for him. And —" She sat up now. "I'm not sure I can handle the... gossip."

He looked vaguely confused. "What?"

"If I'm seen to be fraternizing with the man who donated a billion dollars to our hospital..."

Rafa looked at her askance. "Okay, now you're not making sense. What does that have to do with anything?"

"People could make the link between Thomasina's death, the donation, the accident, you and I..."

"Listen to me. This is crazy talk. Tomi died two years ago, and it had nothing, nothing to do with your accident. Christ, you nearly died! I saw you when they brought you in, Noe—"

"—you saw me?"

Rafa nodded, his eyes on hers. "They let me sit with you for a while until your family could get to you."

Noemi stared at him. "I never knew that."

Rafa smiled sheepishly. "I don't think your sister approved of me. She thought it was a conflict of interest. Also, I think she thought... no. I don't know what she thought."

"Leo?" Noemi shook her head. "Leo can be, let's say, judgmental. And protective. But she could have mentioned it."

Rafa cupped her face with his palm. "So...?"

"So, for now... this stays between you and me."

He nodded. The kid was obviously mixed up and who could blame her? He hadn't meant to seduce her—guiltily, he'd recalled that he had been at that bar to meet someone on a blind date a friend had set up.

But his dreams had been haunted by Noemi Castor for so long. "If that's what you want, Noe. You and me. For now."

Noemi leaned in, obviously relieved, and kissed him. "This is a dream, I swear it is."

He drew her close, her soft, pillowy breasts against his chest, her fresh, clean scent in his nostrils and the taste of her skin on his lips. "Then let's keep dreaming. At least for tonight."

"You don't have to get back for Bepi?"

"He's with Tomi's parents for a few days."

Right on cue, Mouse gave a plaintiff whine. She had been shut out of the bedroom long enough. Noemi and Rafa laughed. "Hold that thought, gorgeous man."

Mouse leaped onto the bed as soon as Noemi opened the door and curved her furry body into Rafa's. Noemi made a face at her dog. "Such a slut, Mousie."

Rafa grinned at her and patted his other side. "I'm greedy, I want two beautiful girls next to me."

Because of Mouse's presence, they didn't make love again, but chatted until Noemi fell asleep.

Rafa lay awake, gazing at her perfect face. He wondered whether he was doing the right thing; she was so young, so vulnerable, and yet it seemed impossible that they couldn't be together. Making love to her had been sublime, exhilarating—just being inside her, he was in heaven.

But he could tell the young woman in his arms was damaged, and knowing he was as damaged... was this responsible?

Maybe he should concentrate on getting Noemi's head right before he looked at himself. Or was that overstepping?

"Hell, I don't know," he whispered. Before Tomi, he'd always been terrible at figuring out relationships.

He tightened his arms around Noemi. They'd figure it out. He couldn't imagine his life without her now.

. . .

THE MAN outside the woman's apartment waited but Rafael Genova did not emerge. So, he was sleeping with the pretty girl—he wondered who she was.

It didn't matter. If she got in the way, then she'd suffer the same fate as Genova.

Time's up, beautiful people, he thought, and got back into his car, driving away into the Seattle night.

CHAPTER NINE

Noemi woke and for a long moment, she just reveled in the feeling of Rafa's arms wrapped around her. She pretended that it wasn't complicated at all—that this was just how things were supposed to be. That they had no other responsibilities other than to hold each other.

She opened her eyes and looked up at her sleeping companion. Rafa's long, thick, dark eyelashes rested on his cheeks as he slept, and at rest, he looked younger than his forty years and less... troubled.

God, he was beautiful. She traced the shape of his lips with her finger and he smiled. The way he looked at her when he opened his eyes made her entire body flush with warmth.

"Good morning." Noemi whispered.

"Good morning, beautiful."

She kissed him. "If we both have morning breath, does it count?"

"Nope." He chuckled and kissed her again. "You okay?"

Noemi nodded. "I am." She smiled a little sheepishly. "Sorry for freaking out on you last night. It was just so unexpected, you know?" She placed her hand on his bare chest. "I'm still not quite believing it."

"Well, it happened." He took her face in his hands. "And I would like it to happen again and again... but I know you have reservations. Look, however you want to handle this is fine by me. Keep it between us? Cool. You need some time? No problem. Just don't push me away." He pressed his lips to hers tenderly. "I turned away from you once. I'll always regret it."

They made love again slowly and then luxuriously showered together. Afterward, Noemi made them both eggs. "I'm not much of a cook."

Rafa put a forkful into his mouth, and Noemi giggled as she saw him try to arrange his face into something other than revulsion. "Told you." She took his plate away. "I can do toast."

"Or we could go out for breakfast. No?"

Noemi gave a nervous smile. "I live close to the hospital..."

"Gotcha. Then toast is fine, baby. Listen, do you have to be at work today?"

She shook her head and Rafa smiled. "Good. Want to spend the day together? We can stay in or go out of the city."

"I'd like that."

RAFA DROVE them out of the city, down towards Mount Rainier, and they hiked along a light mountain trail with Mouse. Noemi usually loved exploring, but today her attention was wholly absorbed by this man. She realized that even with all the time spent with him and Thomasina, she barely knew him.

Rafael Genova had always seemed quiet, tranquil, and even a little aloof. This Rafa, however, was fun, goofy—and God, she adored him. He held her hand as they walked, his thumb stroking the back of her hand. His smile lit up his face. He teased her about her walking prowess. "Come on, young 'un," he said in his best Grandpa voice when she moaned about being tired.

"You exhausted me last night," she giggled and yelped as he tickled her.

"Baby, if you think that was exhausting, just wait... that was nothing."

Noemi caught her breath as he took her tightly in his arms, and he kissed her so passionately, her head whirled. "You better keep that promise, Mr. Genova."

"Oh, believe me, I will," he murmured, and pleasure flooded her body. His green eyes were fixed intensely upon hers. "There isn't anything I won't do to you if you let me, beautiful girl."

After that, she couldn't wait to get home. In the car on the way back to Seattle, she slid her hand onto his groin and stroked him through his pants. Rafa smiled at her. "Tease."

"Punish me later," she quipped gently, but the thought of him dominating her made her sex flood with wetness, and she licked her lips slowly.

When they were back at her apartment, she pressed her body against his. "Rafa... do whatever you want to me. I want you in every way."

Rafa crushed his lips against hers, pressing her against the wall. His hands went to the zipper of her pants and tugged it open. Noemi tore at his clothes.

They never made it to the bedroom. Rafa fucked her hard on the hallway floor, making her scream as she came, then she straddled him and rode him, completely uninhibited.

She urged him to blindfold her or tie her up, whatever he wanted, just so that she could feel like she was his in every way. Every mental wall she had ever built came tumbling down as they spent the next two days making love and talking and laughing.

Loving.

AT THE END of their time together, those few days that they had been able to devote to each other, reality inevitably set in. There was Bepi to consider, plus their families and their work. Rafa kissed her before he left to pick his son up. "I guess this is where we start to figure out the future."

"I guess so."

"Can I call you later?"

Noemi grinned. "Do you even have to ask?"

THE APARTMENT FELT empty without Rafa in it. Even Mouse sniffed around the rooms looking for him. "I know how you feel, boo," Noemi told her dog, and then she grabbed the dog's leash. "Come on! Let's go walk it off... grab your ball, Mousie."

She walked the dog for what seemed like hours, then as she returned to her street, she saw two of her neighbors outside on the sidewalk. She greeted them, and they turned to her.

"Noemi... we've called the police."

"What's up?"

"Sweetheart, we think someone broke into your home. We heard a commotion, and of course, we went to investigate. Joseph went in and someone hit him."

Noemi was horrified. "Oh my God! Is he okay?"

Phyllis, the elder of the two women, nodded. "He's okay—just a little shocked. Ruby is taking care of him. Anyway, whoever was in your apartment got away..."

Noemi felt sick. "Are you sure Joe's alright?"

"Oh yes, dear. But Noe, I wouldn't go into your apartment until the police get here," Phyllis put her hand on Noemi's arm as Noemi moved towards the building. "We don't know if anyone else is in there, dear."

THE POLICE TOOK their time in her apartment and eventually, the lead officer came out and asked her to accompany them inside. "I'm afraid there has been some vandalism, Doc. We need you to tell us if anything is missing, and I must warn you, someone wanted to leave a message. You might find it a little distressing."

Noemi had no idea what that could be until she saw the word scrawled in paint across her wall and her heart sank.

Whore.

CHAPTER TEN

Ally's eyes were huge. "Oh, God, Noe, that's awful. Do the police have any clues?"

"None—and nothing was taken. They're working on the presumption that it was a junkie who must have known I was a doctor and who tried to find any drugs I might have stashed." Noemi rolled her eyes.

"But still... I'm glad you have Mouse now. God." Ally looked sick, and Noemi hugged her.

"I'm fine, Al, don't worry." She let her friend go and changed into her scrubs. Noemi had decided not to tell anyone about the 'Whore' message that had been scrawled on her wall, but inside, her nerves were frayed. It could well have been a disgruntled junkie, disappointed that she wasn't some clinician who stole from her workplace and therefore couldn't provide him with the fix he needed.

But coming so soon after her wonderful few days with Rafael Genova, it seemed too coincidental. After the police had given her the all clear, she had spent the previous evening scrubbing the message off her wall and repainting the whole thing.

She hadn't told Rafa either. He had called at ten that night, Bepi having been read to and tucked in, and they had talked for a while.

"I wish you were here with me," he said gently.

"Me too, but we have all the time in the world. We have to do this right for all our sakes, Rafa."

"I know."

So, Noemi had decided to not say anything to anyone, not even Ally. For now, her tryst with Rafa would stay her secret. But he dominated her thoughts every moment when she wasn't concentrating on her work and her patients.

At lunch, she sat at their table, thinking of Rafa's lips on hers when Kit nudged her. "Hey you."

"Hey, KitKat."

Kit grinned. They had fallen very quickly back into the pattern of teasing they had enjoyed in Syria, and Noemi was glad to have her friend around. Not as glad as Ally, Noemi grinned to herself, knowing Ally and Kit were hooking up and loving it. She was glad for them both.

"Listen," Kit said, dragging a chair next to hers. "I've got someone who wants to meet you. Drew Ballentine? Thomasina Ballentine's stepbrother. I think I told you I knew him?"

"You did. I'm actually surprised I never met him; I met most of the family."

"Pretty sure there was some family stuff going on. Dang, I don't know, family politics? Anyhoo, I ran into him the other day, and he said he'd love to meet you. To thank you for taking care of Thomasina."

Noemi looked away from Kit's gaze. "He doesn't need to do that."

"Noe." Kit glared at her. "Stop that."

Noemi half-laughed. Kit knew her so well. "Sorry. Bring him by for coffee when it's convenient."

"Good," Kit stole a French fry from her plate. "Because he'll be here this afternoon."

"This afternoon?"

"Come on now, no time like the present and all of that." Kit grinned at her, then seeing her expression, his smile faded. "Noe, it's no big deal. He just wants to say hi."

"Fine."

Kit nudged her. "Hate me?"

"With the fury of a thousand suns." But she couldn't stop grinning as he poked her side. "Bully."

"Wimp."

DREW BALLENTINE WAS nothing like Noemi expected. Dressed expensively in a dark grey suit, he was shorter than she expected—but then he was with the gigantic Kit when she first saw him. Ballentine was still taller than her and had a friendly smile on his face as Kit introduced them. He shook Noemi's hand with both of his.

"I cannot begin to tell you how grateful we all were to you, Dr. Castor. You went above and beyond for our Thomasina. I hope you are completely recovered from your injuries?"

"I am, thank you."

He was so different from Tomi's no-nonsense down-to-earth personality. She soon discovered he was a minister of a small congregation outside of Modesto, California, and she guessed his smooth, practiced routine was part of that persona.

Noemi couldn't make out whether he was genuine or not. She barely remembered Thomasina mentioning her stepbrother and didn't feel comfortable asking Drew questions about his relationship with his stepsister.

He was handsome in a bland way and obviously, he thought he was charming enough. Noemi felt bad about judging him—and realized she was doing so because she couldn't work out why she hadn't met him before.

He appeared genuine and was interested in the clinic which bore his stepsister's name.

Noemi couldn't resist. "I'm surprised you haven't visited before?" Kit shot her a look, but Noemi smoothed her expression out with a friendly smile. No agenda here, buddy.

Drew smiled. "I can see you have questions, Dr. Castor. To be frank... there is a rift in our family, one that I have been working to heal for the past few years. I will always regret not working harder before our dear Thomasina died."

Ah. So that was it. Noemi politely showed him around the clinic, and he made all the right noises of approval.

"My almost-brother-in-law has certainly been generous, not that I'd expect anything else." Drew murmured.

"You know Rafa... Mr. Genova well?"

"Not as well as I would like," Drew inclined his head with a rueful smile. "And I would love to get to know my nephew. I've tried to reach out, but I think, perhaps for him, the wound is still too raw. He loved Thomasina with all his heart, don't you think, Dr. Castor?"

"Yes, he did." Noemi's throat closed. Was there an insinuation in his words?

No, don't be paranoid. He couldn't possibly know about you and Rafa...

"Thomasina was an easy person to love," Noemi said firmly. "An inspiration. The world is a worse place for her not being in it."

Drew Ballantine's face softened, and for the first time, she could see real emotion in his eyes. "Thank you for saying that, Dr. Castor. Bless you."

She smiled tentatively at him. "Will you be in Seattle for long, sir?"

"It's Drew, and yes, I hope for a little while anyway. I hope to see Bepi before I leave, at the very least. Perhaps I can persuade you to join me for coffee one day?"

"Perhaps," Noemi answered noncommittally. "I hate to rush off, but I do have surgeries to get to. It was good to meet you, Mr. Ballantine."

"Drew."

"Drew," she replied, shaking his hand. She smiled at both him and Kit before making her escape.

Ally was waiting for her in the scrub room, having seen her

earlier with Kit and Ballentine. "Do you just attract the handsome ones by magic or what?"

"You mean Tomi's brother? You think he's handsome?"

Ally considered. "He's not my type—"

"—nor mine."

"—but he is a good-looking man. Tomi's brother?"

Noemi nodded. "Stepbrother. He's okay, but there's something... I don't know. Missing."

"Like what?"

Noemi pondered while she scrubbed in. "I don't know," she told Ally. "I can't figure it out."

Kit Vaughan smiled at his acquaintance. "So, what do you think?"

"She's lovely, Kit, just as you said." Drew Ballantine nodded at him.

Kit sat forward. "Look, normally I would never interfere in a friend's life. Ever. But I just feel that Noe needs... I don't know... guidance, absolution, something. She had her confidence shattered, and I hate seeing it. I can't figure it out, and so that's why I came to you. Think you can help her?"

Drew smiled at him, and picking up his coffee, sipped the hot liquid. "Oh, yes," he said softly, "I really do think I can help her."

11

CHAPTER ELEVEN

Noemi didn't tell Rafael about the break-in, but she did tell him she met Drew Ballantine.

"And what did you think of him?" Rafa's voice was even and measured, but she detected a hint of tension. She put down the saucepan of pasta she was about to strain and looked at him.

"I didn't really form much of an opinion except that he appeared very different from Tomi."

Rafa nodded and took the pan, draining it and dumping the pasta into a dish. They were cooking together in his city apartment, a luxurious penthouse in one of Seattle's most exclusive buildings. The view over Elliott Bay was breathtaking, but Noemi knew he hadn't brought her here to impress her. He just wanted her to feel at home.

Mouse, for whom Rafa had bought a new dog bed, was fast asleep in the living room as they took their supper in, balancing plates on their knees and sitting on the couch to eat and talk. "I don't know him that well myself; I just know the situation with the family. Ballentine's father was only married to Tomi's mom for a few years."

"He didn't come to see Tomi when she was sick."

"No." Rafa's expression told Noemi what he was feeling. She touched his arm.

"Hey look, he may have had a good reason. Did Tomi say anything about him?"

Rafa sighed and put his plate down on the coffee table. "Not really. I know there was some friction because her mom adores Drew, him being a God-fearing preacher and Tomi being the rebel. But Tomi never resented Drew; they were just two wildly different people."

Noemi studied him. "But you're not a fan?"

Rafa shrugged. "Look... I'm no angel, and I'm biased because I think that regardless of temperament, he should have been there for Tomi. But, as I say, I might be a little unfair to the man. I only met him a couple of times."

Noemi chuckled a little. "Families, huh?"

"Preach, sister. Did you always get along with your sister?"

Noemi hooted. "Hell, no. When we were growing up, we used to fight nonstop. Real brawls too. Ma and Pa used to have to physically restrain us. We're too much alike; that's mine and Leo's problem. Very judgey and convinced we're right all the time."

Rafa grinned. "Oh, dear God, what have I got myself into?"

"I'm afraid it's way too late for regrets, Genova," Noemi laughed and leaned over to kiss him. "Excuse my garlic breath."

"Ditto." He kissed her again and smiled. "Siblings are strange creatures. They share the same DNA and yet sometimes—"

He trailed off, and Noemi saw something in his eyes: a reluctance, a distant memory he did not want to conjure. "What is it? Is it your brother?"

Rafa sighed. "Zani's been off the rails for years. I love him, but he's... there's some sort of personality disorder going on there, I'm convinced. He seems to be missing that sensitivity part."

"Like a sociopath?"

"Exactly that. He loves money, women, and himself." Rafa shook his head. "Maybe I am being too harsh. I haven't seen or heard from him in so long."

"And your parents?"

"Nope. Mom tries to reach out to him, but she gets nowhere."

Rafa shrugged. "I think she sees Bepi as the son she wanted to have—not that she overmothers him. She was always very respectful of Tomi's motherhood." He suddenly smiled. "Even if Tomi was a little too, um, liberal in her ways for her."

Noemi laughed. "Wasn't she? I really enjoyed that rebellious streak about her."

"Me too."

LATER, as they watched a movie together, her head on his chest, Noemi wondered that they could talk so easily of Tomi, and it felt so separate from their own relationship. *Would you approve, Tomi? Would you approve of Rafa and I? Or would you see it as a final insult?*

Noemi felt Rafa's fingers stroking through her hair. The way he made her feel, he was intoxicating. His touch made every cell in her body react, and Noemi didn't know if that meant her reason disappeared when she was with him, and whether that was healthy.

"Noe?"

She looked up to see him smiling at her. "Yes?"

"You're overthinking things."

"How do you know?"

He grinned. "You grind your teeth. This side." He touched her face just in front of her ear. "Let's just enjoy our time together and not worry about anything. Can we do that?"

"Sorry. Of course."

"Good." He kissed her, and as the kiss intensified, his arms tightened around her. Noemi's hands slid under his sweater, stroking his hard stomach, feeling the muscles contract under her touch.

"Take me to bed, Genova."

Rafa chuckled, a deep sound that rumbled through his chest. "Actually, I was thinking I'd like to have you on the rug..."

He tumbled her to the floor, making Noemi giggle as he pretended to munch down on her neck. "Oh, you silly man."

She could barely believe there were so many years between them;

she felt no distance despite the ten-year difference. She would never have guessed that he was so much fun, so goofy, but thinking back to when she had first met him, it made sense.

In the hospital, that first time with Thomasina, Rafa had been quiet, even somewhat aloof despite his politeness. Thomasina had regaled everyone with stories and jokes; Rafa had been the one to ask the hard questions.

Now though, Noemi was finding out that Rafa could be playful, too, and now as he undressed her, he would tease and tickle her so that by the time the lovemaking begun, they both were relaxed. She loved that about him.

She mussed his dark curls as he pushed down the cup of her bra to take her nipple into his mouth. Noemi sighed, closing her eyes and squirming with pleasure as his tongue flicked around each nipple in turn.

Then his lips were trailing down her belly, his tongue circling her navel. "Open those sweet thighs for me, baby," he murmured, and she obeyed, her clit already expecting his touch, quivering and pulsing with desire.

"You taste like heaven," he said as his tongue dipped deep inside her, and Noemi pulled gently on his hair. Since they met, his dark curls had gone from being cut short and neat, to growing wild about his head, and she loved them.

"Baby, can I taste you too?"

A chuckle, then he moved around. Noemi unzipped his pants and freed his cock from his underwear. She took him into her mouth, sliding her tongue along the thick, heavy length of it. She heard him groan as she began to pleasure him.

They moved with each other, building the tension between them. Noemi shook her head when he asked if she wanted him to pull out before he came, and shortly after, he climaxed, shooting thick cum into her mouth.

She swallowed him down, and then his lips were on hers, and he was hitching her legs around his waist, as she rolled the condom down his cock. When he thrust into her, Noemi gasped and moaned as they began to move with each other. Making love with him was exhilarating, and she lost herself in it. As she came, crying out his name again and again, she arched her back and let out a shuddering cry.

They collapsed on the rug, laughing and panting for air. As Rafa withdrew, he cursed. "Damn it."

"What?"

"The condom split."

Noemi sat up. "Don't worry about it; I'm on birth control." She smiled shyly. "And I haven't any STDs we need to worry about. You?"

"Nope."

"I thought not, but we can never be too careful." She touched his face. "Kind of ruins the romance to talk about it, but I am a doctor after all."

Rafa grinned. He pulled her to her feet. "Well, let's go clean off in the shower, doc, and then I'm gonna show you some more of my sweet moves."

Noemi laughed as he swept her up into his arms, and then shrieked as he turned a very cold shower on her. "You fiend!" She tugged him in beside her and soaked him. Rafa protested, cranking the hot water on. "Serves you right," Noemi chuckled.

They kissed as they soaped each other's bodies, teasing and laughing as they showered together.

"Stay the night."

Noemi was pulling on her sneakers and smiled at Rafa. "I can't. Not tonight. I have to be at the hospital in a couple of hours and if I stay here, there's no way I'm leaving you behind, all alone and warm in that bed."

He laughed. "I'm glad to hear it. Listen, I know you want to keep us low-key... but how would you feel about us meeting with Bepi and taking Mouse for a long walk? I just want Bepi to start getting used to you being around, is all."

Noemi considered. "I guess... I mean, I can see the sense in it."

Rafa was studying her. "But you have reservations."

"What if someone saw us?"

Rafa's smile was fading. "I get it. Listen, let's drop it."

She went to him. "I want to spend time with you and Bepi but it's just too soon, you know?"

"At least come have dinner at the house with us."

"That I can do."

"Tomorrow night?"

"Tomorrow night."

CHAPTER TWELVE

But the next day at work, she took a call from a frantic Leonora. "What's up?"

"It's Jack. He collapsed at Tee Ball, and we took him to the medical center, but they said it was nothing. Healthy kids don't just collapse, Noe."

"Breathe, Leo. Bring him here and I'll check him out, I promise."

Noemi wasn't unduly worried until she saw her nephew: the young boy's skin was tinged blue, and when Noemi checked his fingernails, the beds were almost purple.

"Okay," she said, her calm exterior belying the panic building inside her. "We're just going to run some tests, slugger." She smiled at her sister. Leonora was chewing relentlessly on her bottom lip and watching every one of Noemi's reactions, looking for any clue to her son's condition.

Unfazed, Jack grinned at his aunt. "Cool."

"Can you tell me how it felt when you passed out, Jackie?"

"I just got real tired, and my chest felt tight. I didn't realize I'd passed out until I heard Mom screaming."

"Drama queen." Noemi winked at her nephew, who giggled. Leonora sighed.

"Noe, can I talk to you outside?"

In the hallway, Noemi fixed her sister with a steady look. "We're running tests, Leo. For now, there's nothing more to think about than that."

"I saw your face, Noe. Tell me the truth."

"I don't know anything until I run the tests, Leo." Noemi said firmly. "His color is a little concerning, but we'll figure it out. Come on now, you know I can't tell you anything until we know for sure. Let's not make things worse by panicking."

FINN WAS at her side as they performed an echocardiogram; Noemi was glad of it when they saw the problem.

"Oh, Goddamn it." Noemi looked at the scan of her nephew's heart. "It looks like ASD."

Finn nodded. ASD—Atrial Septal Defect—otherwise known as a hole in the heart. He put his hand on Noemi's shoulder. "Okay, kiddo. First, let's make sure, and then—I'm sorry, but you'll have to take a backseat. You know the rules about treating family."

"Fuck that," Noemi said, "if Jack needs surgery..."

"I will perform the surgery, Noe. Come on now, don't make me pull rank. Besides, we don't know yet whether he'll need it. Let's do this step-by-step."

Noemi felt numb as they went through all the procedures but finally, they all knew. Jack would need surgery and soon. Noemi was incensed when Finn told her she would not even be allowed to assist him, but Leonora calmed her sister down. Noemi shook her head.

"I'm supposed to be the one reassuring you."

"Finn knows what he is doing. After your accident, he spent a lot of time with us explaining your surgeries. I trust him."

"And you don't trust me?" Noemi knew she was being unreasonable. Leo put her arm around her sister.

"Of course I do. But Jack's sick, and he needs this surgery, and he needs it to be... on autopilot if you like. Emotionless to a certain degree. And I need you here with me. I need you."

Noemi sighed and hugged her sister. "Of course."

She went to call Rafa to tell him she wouldn't be able to make it for dinner. "I'm sorry, baby."

"Please don't apologize, Noe. I hope Jack is okay."

JACK'S SURGERY was scheduled for that night. "Best to get it done," Finn said, with a look at Noemi, who nodded.

"Right."

Noemi and Leonora sat in the Relative's Room. For a while they didn't talk, then Noe looked at her sister. "Hey, I wanted to ask you something."

"Go for it."

"When I was in the accident, you never told me that Rafael Genova sat with me until you all arrived at the hospital."

Leonora's face closed up. "Yes, he did. When we got here, I sent him back to his sick fiancée."

Noemi almost smiled. Here was the judgment she had warned Rafa about. "He was just being a good person, Leo."

"I thought it was inappropriate."

"You'd rather I had been alone?"

"Lazlo was here, Dieter—"

"Yes, because what I'd really want at such a time would be my ex-boyfriend." Noemi couldn't help the resentment that crept into her voice. "Rafa is a good person, a good man."

"You seem to think so. Got a crush?"

Nomi was sure her cheeks were flaming red, but she shook her head. "I'm just saying it was good of him."

"Hmm."

Noemi sighed. She wasn't going to argue the point with her sister —not now. It didn't matter; all that mattered now was that Jack pulled through. She knew from experience that these things came out of the blue, that life was always a risk. She believed in Finn, in his abilities.

Their parents arrived at the hospital to wait with them. Marian and Frank, who had always supported their single-mother daughter and adored their grandson, showed concern on their faces, but like Noemi, used distraction to ease Leonora's nerves.

HOURS PASSED, and an antsy Noemi, with her face covered by a surgical mask, sneaked into the operating theatre. She was soon spotted. Finn sighed. "Noemi, please, I am trying to concentrate here."

"Just tell me how it's going."

"Noe..."

There was something in his voice that made her pulse quicken. "What's wrong?"

"Noemi Castor, do you want me to have security remove you?"

"Finn..."

"Ally, would you please take Dr. Castor outside and physically restrain her if she tries to get back in?"

Noemi sighed. "I'm going. Bully," she added with a chuckle, but when Finn didn't laugh, she knew he was serious. Oh God...

Ally came with her anyway, her dark eyes full of concern. "Noe, go and wait with your family. We're doing everything we can."

NOEMI FELT breathless and knew if she went back to the Relative's Room now, her panicked expression would unsettle her family. Instead, she took the elevator to the roof and stepped out onto it, breathing in the night air. She pulled her phone from her pocket and called Rafa again.

"Hey, baby." Rafa's warm voice was the balm she needed.

"Hey. I just needed to hear your voice. Jack's surgery is taking longer than expected."

"It's never pleasant to have to wait like that. Sure you don't want me to come?"

Noemi smiled. "No, my family is here, and besides, Leo is the one who needs propping up. Rafa... I made the mistake of going to the theater. Finn threw me out, but I got the impression that... Oh, God, what if...?"

"Sweetheart, listen. Jack is in the best hands—you yourself told me that. Trust Finn to do everything he can."

"You're right. How's Bepi?"

Rafa chuckled. "Spoiled by his grandmother—who also gave him way too much sugar. Currently, he's chasing Mouse around the garden."

Noemi giggled. Rafa, who worked mainly from home, had volunteered to take care of Mouse when she was at work, and she was grateful for it. She knew how much Mouse liked being around people, and the dog completely adored Bepi. It took the worry of having to find a sitter for her from Noemi's shoulders—especially now.

"I'd better go back in. I'll call you when I know something."

"Take care, baby."

"You too."

RAFAEL ENDED THE CALL, still smiling. Even after such a short time together, he and Noemi were already a partnership, friends as well as lovers—the other person's rock.

He went to find Bepi in the garden. "Come on, kid. Time for bed."

His heart started to beat fast when he saw a tall figure talking to his son. He darted towards them, heart thumping. Where the fuck was his security? "Hey!"

"Hey yourself, brother."

Rafa slowed down, and he squinted into the dim light. "Zani?"

Zani swung Bepi into his arms and walked towards Rafa, who was astonished at his brother's slender appearance. "Zani... what the hell are you doing here?"

Zani smiled. "You mean how did I get through the seven layers of security you have here? This." He pointed to his face, once so like Rafa's, now quite gaunt and older. "I don't look so different, hey?"

Yes. Yes, you do. Rafa took his son from his brother's arms. "Come inside, Zani. I have to put Bepi to bed."

Zani followed them in, admiring Mouse. "Nice dog."

"It's Nommy's dog." Bepi told him. "She lets me play with him when she's at work."

"Nommy, huh?" Zani's eyes sparkled wickedly as he looked at his brother. "New girlfriend?"

Rafa didn't answer. "Go to the kitchen, Zani. Help yourself to coffee, food, whatever. I'll be down as soon as I can."

"Always the gracious host." Zani mussed Bepi's hair. "'Night, kid. Maybe we can hang out tomorrow, yeah?"

Bepi grinned at him, oblivious to his father's tense stance. "Cool."

Rafa bathed Bepi and put him to bed, spending time to read to him, putting off having to go back downstairs to face his brother. What the hell was Zani doing here? And why hadn't he called before showing up like this?

Rafa thought he knew the answer, but it wasn't until he rejoined Zani that he knew for sure. "So, what brings you back to Seattle?"

Zani smiled. "A job, hopefully. A position back in the family business."

Aha. He'd been right. Zani had finally blown through his fortune, and by the looks of him, most of it spent on booze—or worse. Zani was almost skeletally thin; he looked a decade older than his forty-five, and his once-handsome face seemed now watchful and spiteful.

Rafa made a pot of coffee while Zani studied the contents of the refrigerator. "You got anything in here that isn't kale?"

Rafa tried not to grimace. "Plenty, if you look," he said mildly. "Sit down, I'll make you an omelet. You look like you haven't eaten properly in years."

"I like to stay slim." Zani looked at his brother critically. "Still the pretty boy, I see."

Rafa ignored the jibe. "Do Mom and Dad know you're in town?"

Zani shrugged. "I haven't seen them yet. Not sure of the reception I'd get. I thought maybe you could smooth the transition before I ask Dad for a job."

"Dad's not in charge of hiring and firing," Rafa said, his tone even. "For that, you'd have to come to me."

Zani smirked. "In that case..."

Rafa flipped a perfectly cooked omelet onto a plate and slid it to his brother. "Eat. Drink your coffee. Then you can tell me why you're really back."

RAFA WENT to bed about two a.m. Zani's answers to his questions had been evasive and even aggressive, and Rafa had eventually lost the will to listen. He offered Zani a guest room, which his brother accepted. "We will talk more tomorrow," Rafa warned him. Zani just smiled that infuriating smile of his and slunk off to bed.

Rafa asked himself why he felt so unsettled. He certainly knew it was because he didn't trust Zani's intentions. A job? Zani had never worked a day in his life, and Rafa would bet that he wasn't about to start now. Zani wanted money, position. Rafa wondered what had happened in Europe.

He was just falling asleep when he heard someone knocking at his bedroom door. "Come in."

His security guard stuck his head in, an apologetic look on his face. "I'm sorry to disturb you, sir, but I think you'd better come to the front door. Dr. Castor is here... and I don't think she's okay."

Rafa was up in a flash, and as they both hurried back to the front of the house, he saw her. She was almost bent double with grief as he put his arms around her and carried her in.

For a moment, Noemi just stared at him. Rafa stroked her face and waited. Then, when she spoke, her voice was low, cracked, and full of disbelief. "He died, Rafa. Jack. He actually died."

CHAPTER THIRTEEN

S lowly, Noemi told him what had happened. When Finn had opened the child's chest, they'd tried to fix the hole in Jack's heart. Although the surgery had progressed well, Jack had stroked out on the table. Finn fought to get him back, but Jack was too far gone.

A shell-shocked Finn had come to tell them that Jack was gone. Noemi would never forget her sister's terrible howl of grief. Leonora had collapsed screaming, and Frank and Marian had tried to comfort her.

Noemi had darted from the room, running, running to the operating theater, her mind fixed on saving Jack, doing everything she could... There must be a way, there must be a way...

Ally, tears streaking down her face, had managed to stop her after Noemi burst into the room, seeing her nephew lying so still on the table, being cared for the theater staff. "Noemi... he's gone, he's gone..."

"No... no..."

Finn had followed her, knowing what she would do; between he and Lazlo, they managed to drag her away. When she finally returned to the Relative's Room and her family, Leo had looked up at her with pleading eyes. Then when Noemi slowly shook her head, Leo in her bottomless sorrow, had screamed and slapped her sister hard. Frank locked his arms around his oldest daughter while Lazlo and Marian tended to a shocked Noemi.

Her retelling to Rafa finished, Noemi began shivering. Rafa drew her into his arms, kissing her temple. "I'm so sorry, baby."

"How can it be? How can he be gone?" Noemi shook her head, not comprehending the horror of the last few hours. "From collapsing on a Tee Ball field to the morgue? I don't understand."

Rafa couldn't think of anything to do to comfort her. Instead, he wrapped her in his arms, and they lay together on the couch for what seemed like hours.

"Leo doesn't want me near her. She blames me."

"That's just the grief talking. You're the person closest to her. She knows she can rail at you and that you'll forgive her."

Noemi buried her face in his neck. "Who did you rail at?"

Rafa was silent for a while and she drew away and studied his face. "Who?"

"No one. I couldn't. I had Bepi to think of and Tomi's parents. And it wasn't the same. We knew. We had time. We prepared. When—"

He broke off and shook his head. "We were prepared." He had almost said *when you had your accident and the heart was destroyed,* but that really wasn't what Noemi needed to hear right now. He could see she was absolutely destroyed by Jack's death. "Sweetheart, let me call your folks, let them know where you are."

She shook her head. "No, I'll text them and tell them I'm safe—with a friend."

"Fine." But inwardly he sighed—what did it matter now who knew about them? But Noemi clearly wasn't thinking about anything but her nephew. Rafa persuaded her to go to bed, laying down beside her and holding her. He hadn't expected her to sleep but finally just before dawn, exhausted, she closed her eyes.

· · ·

RAFA'S HEART pounded with sadness for her and for her family. He grabbed a couple of hours of sleep but then he got up to deal with Bepi.

Zani was already up, and Rafa found him in the kitchen, chatting to an excited Bepi. Rafa kissed his son's head and nodded to his brother. "Good morning."

"Morning, bro." Zani grinned at him. "We didn't want to wake you —or your guest."

Rafa sighed. So, Zani had heard what went on last night. Bepi looked at his father questioningly.

"Nommy is here. Now listen, I have something to tell you, and it's very sad." He explained about Jack to Bepi who nodded, his expression sad. "It's our job to make sure Nommy is okay, alright, sport?"

"Okay, Papa."

Rafa looked at Zani, who was listening to them. "Noemi is a friend, a dear friend. She helped us when Thomasina was sick. Mouse is her dog."

Zani's smirk made Rafa want to punch the smile off his face. He'd obviously guessed that Noemi was more than just a 'dear friend'.

Rafa gritted his teeth and made Bepi some breakfast while Zani made coffee.

"Hello."

Rafa turned to see Noemi, her eyes wide and blinking, standing in the doorway. "Hey, lovely. Come on in. Noe, this is Zani, my brother."

Noemi's face registered surprise, and Zani laughed. "My reputation clearly precedes me. Yes, the prodigal son has returned." He went to Noemi and took her hand. "My dear, I'm so sorry about your loss."

"Thank you." Noemi's voice was strangled, and she looked between Rafa and Zani, unsure of what to say to the man. Bepi saved her. He hopped from his chair and went to her, hugging her legs. She picked him up, and he threw his tiny arms around her neck. "Nommy, I am sorry about Jack." He kissed her cheek and squeezed her neck. Noemi's eyes filled with tears, and she hugged the child tightly.

Rafa looked at Zani and nodded out of the room. Give us some privacy. To his relief, Zani nodded and politely excused himself.

"Bepi, come finish your breakfast while I make some coffee for Nommy."

Noemi slotted Bepi back onto his chair. Rafa kissed her cheek. "You didn't have to get up."

"I think I should go to the hospital whether Leo wants me there or not. There might be an autopsy; there'll certainly be an investigation. God, I can't believe I'm even saying this out loud."

Her shoulders slumped, and she turned her head, burying her face in his sweater so Bepi wouldn't see her cry. Rafa held her as Bepi gazed at them, his green eyes scared. "Bepi, pal, go find your uncle, buddy."

Bepi nodded and slid off his chair, disappearing out of the room. Noemi let out a sob and Rafa held her as she cried.

Finally, she drew away. "I'm sorry, you don't need this."

"Hey, hey, hey, stop that. We're a partnership, Noe, we support each other."

She nodded, wiping her face, and tried to smile. "I have to go."

"At least let me drive you."

Noemi shook her head. "No, I have my car. I'm sorry I dumped this on you—I just—I didn't want to go home."

He slid his hands onto her face and kissed her. "Why don't you stay here for a few days? I don't think you should be alone."

Noemi hesitated. "Can I think about it?"

"Of course."

She hugged Mouse. "Do you mind looking after her again? Just for a while?"

"More than happy to, sweetheart." Rafa frowned. Noemi really did look unwell. "Darling, please, let me drive you to work."

In the end, she relented, and he drove her into Seattle. At the hospital, he wanted to offer to come in with her, but he could already see she was ready to run and hide. He kissed her goodbye. "Later. Call me and I'll come pick you up, unless you're with your family. Just... don't shut me out."

"I won't. You've been incredible, Rafa, thank you."

She got out of the car and Rafa had the strangest feeling that he wouldn't see her again. No, don't be paranoid. It's just the heightened emotion.

The next moment, Noemi disproved his point by dashing back to the car, climbing in and kissing him. "I love you," she whispered.

And then she was gone.

CHAPTER FOURTEEN

Noemi chickened out at first and went to hide in the changing rooms. Luckily, it was deserted, and she sank to one of the benches and put her head in her hands. What was she thinking, telling Rafa she loved him—even if it was true?

Now he would just think it was because she was so mired in grief that she couldn't think straight, when Noemi knew with all her heart that she spoke the truth. She did love Rafael Genova—every inch of him.

"Fuck, fuck, fuck."

"Well, if you're offering..."

She jumped, startled, and saw Kit Vaughan smiling at her. He sat down beside her and looped an arm around her, his smile fading, his eyes serious. "Hey, kiddo. I'm so sorry about your nephew."

"Everyone knows?"

"Yeah. Word got around. Your sister is still here with your mom and dad. We all tried to get them to go home and get some sleep, but they wouldn't leave Jack."

"Are they taking care of him?"

"Of course, babe. Look, there will be an M&M, you know the drill, but Finn's going to be handling it."

"Are they doing an autopsy?"

Kit nodded, and Noemi groaned. "I know they need to, but God, Kit. He was just a kid. Six years old. Six."

"Which is why we need to know how he stroked out on us." He cleared his throat, and Noemi realized he had more to say.

"What?"

"Noe... Children's Services got involved."

Noemi was aghast. "Why?"

"They say that there may be a case for neglect."

"Are you fucking kidding me?" Noemi was on her feet now. "Leo was the best fucking mother on the planet... how fucking dare they?" She was screaming now, her temper overwhelming her. "There were no symptoms until there were symptoms! If anyone was negligent, it's that fucking medical center that sent him home... Jesus, if it hadn't been for Leo..."

"Jack would still be dead."

Noemi whirled around to see her sister, her eyes hooded and ringed with black circles, leaning on the door jamb. Leo looked at Kit, who nodded and slipped from the room, squeezing Leo's shoulder on the way out. Leo looked at Noemi. "I'm sorry I hit you, Noe. I'm really sorry. None of this is your fault... I lost it."

Noemi went to her sister, and they embraced. "You can hit me all you want, Leo, if it makes you feel better."

Leo gave a half-laugh, half-sob. "I keep thinking I'll wake up, and none of this will be true. That I'll get up and Jack will already be in the kitchen, mixing his cereals up in that way that used to make me crazy and grinning at me. How is it that will never happen again? How is that possible?"

"I wish I knew, Leo. I can barely believe it myself. I see things like this all the time, and yet—the unfairness of it, the brutality, the shock of it. God."

She hugged her sister tightly then let her go, both women wiping their tears away. "Are Mom and Dad still here?"

Leo shook her head. "I made them go home." She sighed and

rubbed her hand over her face. "I was worried about you, about where you'd gone."

Noemi looked away. "I was with a friend." She could feel Leo's scrutiny and she sighed. "It's Rafael Genova, okay? We've been seeing each other."

Leonora's face went still. "Oh."

"Yeah. It's still very new. Look, this is hardly the time to talk about my sex life, Leo. Come on, let's go grab something to eat, and then you really need to lie down."

To her relief, Leo let Noemi steer her to the cafeteria and make her eat some breakfast and drink coffee. Noemi found a room she could sleep in for a few hours.

"I don't want Jack to be alone," Leo fretted but Noemi reassured her.

"I'll go be with him, Leo. I promise."

IN THE MORGUE, the attendant gave her a sympathetic look and directed her to where Jack lay under a sheet. "I'm so sorry, Dr. Castor."

Noemi found herself trembling as she lifted the sheet and looked at the too-still face of her beloved nephew. Memories came flooding back of family holidays, birthdays, Christmases... she had been with Leo in the delivery room when she gave birth to Jack.

Noemi had no tears left. The pain of his death was so overwhelming she wondered if any of them would ever be happy again. This morning, seeing Bepi, a knife had twisted in her gut, and she'd almost ran away out of the house.

But she hadn't. She needed Rafa at that moment, more than ever and when she had told him that morning that she loved him, she had meant it with all her heart.

Noemi dragged a chair over to the gurney and sat down, holding Jack's cold hand in hers. She didn't know how long she sat there, but she started when a hand was placed on her shoulder. "Hey, Noemi."

She looked up. Donald, the kind-faced pathologist was smiling down at her. "I'm so sorry, Noe, but it's time. We have to take him down now."

"Can I come with him?"

Donald looked uncomfortable. "No, sweetheart, you know that's not permitted."

"I promised his mom I wouldn't let him be alone."

"I'll stay with him." They both looked around to see Ally, her face blotchy from crying. She had known and loved Jack too. "I'll go in with him, Noe."

Noemi nodded, and they took Jack down to the autopsy room. She went back upstairs. She knew Lazlo wouldn't allow her to work today, but she felt like she would go mad if she didn't find anything to do. She checked in on Leo, still sleeping, and called her parents. They were still in shock.

"Sweetie, just look after Leo for us, would you? You know she doesn't blame you; it was just the emotion."

Noemi reassured her parents that she and Leo were fine. She went down to find some coffee, and as she sipped it, she saw Finn. He looked devastated, and she went to him. "It wasn't your fault."

Finn shook his head. "You can say that, but it won't make any difference in how I feel."

Noemi hugged him. "I know how that feels, Finn, I really do."

THE WEIGHT of the grief was overwhelming, and Noemi felt as if she were swimming in treacle with it. As she waited for the results of the autopsy, she went to see Lazlo. He didn't seem surprised when she asked for some time off.

"Of course, Noe, that's not a problem. But keep in touch, won't you? I'll worry."

The results of the autopsy showed that Finn had done everything he could, but it was just damn bad luck that Jack stroked out. Leo took the news calmly. "So, there was really nothing anyone could have done."

"Nothing."

Leo tried to smile. "It doesn't make me feel better."

"What could? Come on, boo, let's go to Mom and Dad's. They'll want to know."

Leo rubbed her eyes. "I have to arrange the funeral home."

Noemi bit her lip. "I've done it for you. I hope that was okay... it can be changed if you want. I just wanted to take that off your plate, to save you the details, but if I've overstepped—"

Leo shook her head. "No. Thank you, Noe."

"We'll go meet them in the morning. They're going to take Jack soon. We'll wait until he leaves then we'll go home, yes?"

THEIR PARENTS WELCOMED them with hugs but no words. There was nothing else to be said, after all. Noemi waited until her family went to bed before going outside into the cold night air. She sat on the front porch swing and called Rafa. "Hey, baby."

"Hey, beautiful, how are you?"

"Sad. Listen... I didn't mean to freak you out this morning."

Rafa gave a low chuckle. "You didn't. For what it's worth, I feel the same way, but I don't want to say the words over the phone."

A small curl of warmth settled in her frozen body. "God, how did you get through this intact, Rafa? It's unbearable."

"I know, baby, and the answer is... I have no idea. One foot in front of the other, one breath after the last. The pain never leaves you—I won't lie to you. But it... dims. Becomes such a part of the fabric of your soul that you learn to live with it."

Noemi closed her eyes. "It's like acid at the moment."

"I know, babe. But it gets, if not better, then it gets... livable. Ugh, that sounds wrong, but it does."

Noemi smiled down the phone. "You are the most wonderful man," she said softly. "How's Bepi?"

"He's fine, excited because his feckless uncle is here." She could hear the resentment in Rafa's voice.

"Is he really that bad?"

"In the scheme of things, no. But that's the right word: scheme.

Zani's blown his share of the trust fund, and now he wants money. He's asking for a job."

"And you don't want to employ him?"

Rafa sighed. "If I don't, he'll go to Dad and leech from him until Dad's broke. At least if I give Zani something to do, I can make sure he does it."

"But?"

"I don't trust him, Noe. There's something going on with him I'm not getting. Ah, Jesus. I'm sick of talking about Zani. I miss you."

Noemi chuckled. "Me too, baby. Listen, after the funeral, I'll have more time for us. I'm taking some personal time."

"Then if your family can spare you, maybe we could get away, just the two of us."

"I'd like that."

SHE SAID good night and sat outside for a while longer, trying to breathe in as much fresh air as she could. It had been a hellish few years, but this was the worse feeling yet. She had to trust in what Rafa was telling her—that it would become bearable if not healed. At the moment, she couldn't see how.

NOEMI DIDN'T SEE the man watching her from the street across from the house. He took in the soft curves of her figure, the sweetness of her face, even as sad as she looked. She was lovely, truly lovely.

It was such a shame she was involved with the Genova family.

"What a waste," he whispered to himself. "What a truly shameful waste. Run, beautiful girl. Run far away from that family before it destroys you."

CHAPTER FIFTEEN

Noemi ripped another package open and drew out the small plastic stick. The third one in less than a half hour. This couldn't be happening—not now, not today of all days. She did the test again, lining it up on the sink with the last two and waited.

The telltale second blue line showed up again. "Oh, no, no, no..."

Pregnant. How the fuck had this happened? She gave a hollow laugh. Really, Doc? You need a biology lesson? She was on birth control, yes, but she knew as well as anyone it didn't always work and now... now she was pregnant with Rafael Genova's child.

And she'd found out the day, the very day her beloved nephew was being buried. Oh God...

"Noe? You done in there? I'm about to pee myself."

Noemi swept the pregnancy tests and the packaging into her purse and zipped it, flushing the toilet. "Sorry, boo. Daydreaming."

Leo, who looked more together than Noemi had expected, smiled at her as she went to the sink to wash her hands. "Same old Noe."

"Always." Noemi waited until Leo had used the bathroom and followed her sister out, her mind whirling. Forget it for today. One day will make no difference. Today is just about Jack.

"Noe, I wanted to say before we go down, that you chose the funeral home perfectly. Jack looks like he's sleeping. Thank you... thank you."

Noemi's eyes filled with tears, and she hugged her sister tightly. "He is so beautiful, Leo. And you were the best mom. He was so happy all his life, and that was because of you."

Leonora's tears were flowing freely. "I always wondered if I did him a disservice by not keeping his father in his life."

"It was just the opposite. Although Paul was a good man, he wasn't a father. Jack didn't need anyone else but you."

"And you and Mom and Dad. I could never have done it without you." Leonora sighed. "Paul's here, you know. He's broken up." She gave a sob.

Noemi wiped her tears. "Come on, before we both disintegrate into puddles."

As they walked into the chapel, it was full of their friends and family. Paul, Jack's biological father, was leaning over his son's open casket, weeping inconsolably. Noemi couldn't help but think—where were you in the last six years? But she knew she was being harsh. Leo and Paul had parted amicably before Jack was even born, and Jack had never known that Paul, who he'd only met on a few occasions, was even his father.

At the back of the church, Noemi saw Rafa and Bepi, quietly taking their seats, and she smiled at them. Bepi was adorable in his little suit, and Rafa smiled back at her, raising his eyebrows, asking her silently if she was okay. Noemi nodded and touched her chest over her heart. Rafa did the same. The simple gesture made her feel stronger.

The funeral went off slowly and beautifully, and as they laid Jack to rest, Leo stayed strong. "Goodbye, beautiful boy. You will always be with me."

· · ·

THEY HELD the wake at their parent's home. Leo thanked all the guests personally, even Rafa. She stroked Bepi's chubby little cheek. "He's adorable, Rafa."

Rafa gripped her hand. "You need anything—anything—please just ask."

"Thank you." Leo nodded at him and moved away, but then turned and came back. "All I want is... look after my sister. Do that and I'll be happy."

"I promise with all my heart," Rafa said, and Leo nodded and half-smiled.

"I believe you mean that. Thank you, Rafael. See you again, Bepi."

Bepi reached out his little hand and put his fingers on her face. Noemi watched as a million emotions flooded her sister's face before she nodded and walked away. Noemi slipped her hand into Rafa's. "Let's go find somewhere to talk."

Bepi was commandeered by Marian, who, struggling with her grandson's loss, wanted to hug the little boy so badly it hurt. Bepi, always sensitive to emotions around him, threw his arms around her neck and snuggled in tight.

"He's a cute kid."

Noemi turned to see Paul behind her. "Paul..."

Paul shook his head. "I know. Me too. I just wish... I wish I had been a better man. A father. But it's too late now." The depth of sorrow in his eyes was searing.

Noemi had to look away, and she excused herself, pushing her way through the guests and outside with Rafa following her.

They sat down on the porch, and Rafa wrapped his arms around her, pressing his lips to her temple. "I love you, Noemi Castor," he murmured. "I know it's crazy fast, and I know we're declaring this at a time of heightened emotion, but I'm in love with you."

"As I am in love with you, Rafa. So much. I just wish it wasn't so bathed in loss: yours, mine, ours."

"We will get through this, I swear. We've been tested, sure, but I know we belong together."

Noemi smiled at him and kissed his mouth. "I believe we do." She hesitated. The words seemed to want to come out—I'm pregnant, I'm pregnant—but she couldn't do it. Not today. Not here.

LEO MADE NOEMI GO HOME with Rafa. "You need some looking after, and Mom and Dad are fussing around me. I need some time alone too. Go, be with him."

"You approve of him now?"

Leo half smiled. "Let's just say I'm touched he came to the funeral. And that kid is adorable."

She even hugged Rafa before they left and gave him a look. "Remember what I said."

"I promise."

IN THE CAR, Noemi asked him what Leonora had meant. Rafa grinned over at her. "She told me to look after you."

Noemi chuckled. "Ah, Leo. Feminism passed you by, didn't it?"

"Hey now, I need looking after too. Isn't that what feminism is? Equality?" Rafa stuck his tongue in his cheek, and Noemi giggled. It felt so good to laugh. Noemi looked around at Bepi, fast asleep in his child's seat.

"He looks so adorable in that little suit. Did you get it off the rack or did you have it tailored for him in Italy?" She teased Rafa but when he looked sheepish, she gasped.

"Seriously? Your four-year-old son has his suits tailored in Italy?"

Rafa chuckled. "Now you sound like Tomi. But yeah, he needs a suit so every birthday, he gets measured, and I have one made. It's kind of like a family tradition. My dad used to do it for Zani and me when we were growing up. My mom still has every one of them in her 'archive'. Yes, she has an 'archive' of my baby clothes."

Noemi was giggling. "Oh, how the rich live. When I was growing up the only tradition I knew was fighting over the turkey wishbone on Thanksgiving."

Rafa smiled at her. "You've never talked about your upbringing. Do you remember your birth parents?"

"Not at all. I was still a baby when the Castors adopted me, so I've never known any other life or any other family. I have no need or drive to find my birth family. I was so lucky. All I know is my father was African-American and my mom was Creole from New Orleans. Even growing up mixed race in a white family—nothing seemed out of place. I was with the people I was supposed to be with."

"And you were close with Leo?"

Noemi smiled. "I am. As soon as I was able to communicate, we've been best friends. We share the same sense of mischief. I used to do this thing in the schoolyard while we were playing: I'd holler like a banshee and where ever she was, she'd banshee me back. Best friends. Since then we've fought and played, and I could not imagine being closer to someone who actually shared my DNA."

Rafa reached over and took her hand. "That's a hell of a story. I love it. I often wondered about what it would be like to have a sister instead of a brother."

"Were you and Zani close?"

He shook his head. "Not really. Too different."

BACK AT RAFA'S Lake Washington mansion, Zani was nowhere to be found. Rafa put a sleeping Bepi to bed, then he and Noemi went to his bedroom. They undressed and got into his bed. Rafa stroked her hair back from her face. "Are you tired, baby?"

She shook her head, her gaze meeting his, and they kissed, their lips soft at first, but as the tension built, rougher, hungrier. Noemi needed him tonight, needed to make love to blank out the sadness of the day, and as he gently moved her onto her back, she tangled her fingers in his hair, pulling his lips to hers. "Don't wait... don't wait."

She wrapped her legs around him and he slid into her. Noemi rocked her hips up to meet him, never taking her eyes from his gaze, pouring all her emotion into making love to this wonderful man.

Rafael braced his arms either side of her head and began to thrust hard, both of them breathing hard. "I love the way your body moves when we fuck," he said, his voice gruff with desire, and she smiled, wriggling beneath him, making her breasts jiggle. Rafa grinned.

"God, you're beautiful," he said, kissing her hard enough that they both tasted blood. It only made their lovemaking more intense as they clawed at each other, leaving marks on each other's skin.

"Cum on my belly," Noemi gasped as he withdrew, shooting thick, creamy semen onto her skin as he came, groaning her name. Noemi reached her own peak, arching her back up as he gathered her to him, watching her as she shivered and moaned with pleasure.

"Christ, Noe..." His lips were trailing down her body, his hand massaging his cum into her skin. His mouth found her nipples as Noemi caught her breath, panting hard as she came down from the high.

Rafa didn't let her rest, though; in minutes, he was inside her again, pushing her knees to her chest, slamming his hips against her as his thick, long, rock-hard cock plunged relentlessly inside her. Noemi came again and again until finally, they both collapsed on the bed, panting hard, laughing.

"God, I needed that... is it me or does it just keep getting better... and better..." She rolled over to kiss him, and he cupped her face in his hands.

"It isn't just you... that was unbelievable."

Noemi grinned at him. "Your cock is the stuff of legend."

Rafa laughed. "You mean Derek?"

"No, you did not name your cock Derek." Noemi burst into giggles and slid her hand down to stroke 'Derek.' "He's at least a Thor. Or a Loki. No, I know, he's Mjolnir."

Rafa shook his head. "I wish I knew what the hell you were talking about, young person."

"Ha, don't try to convince me you're not a comics geek, Genova."

Rafa grinned. "You got me. So, by the way you're wielding 'Mjolnir', I'm assuming you, Dr. Castor, are now claiming to be Thor?"

Noemi, chuckling, straddled him and drew the tip of his cock up and down her damp sex. "I don't think Thor ever did this with his hammer." She lowered herself onto him, taking him in deep, and they made love again. Rafa's hands were rough on her body, and she urged him to be firm with her, grabbing her wrists hard, digging his fingers into the soft flesh of her hips.

"You keep encouraging me like that," Rafa breathed hard, desire igniting in his eyes, "and we're going to have to do some experimentation."

Noemi felt her cunt flood with desire at his words, and he chuckled. "Oh, you like that idea? Want me to tie you up, Princess?"

She nodded and Rafa smiled. "Maybe we should get some leather straps, some other toys..."

Noemi moaned, riding him harder as he described what he'd like to do to her in graphic detail.

Afterwards, she lay down beside him, and he kissed her forehead. "We can do it all, baby. All of it. Whatever, whenever. I want to experience everything with you."

So INVOLVED WERE they in their lovemaking, they didn't notice Zani in the shadows watching them from the doorway. His eyes slid over Noemi's lush body, her café-au-lait skin covered in a fine dewy glow, her breasts and belly undulating as she breathed hard.

Desire twisted in his gut, and he slid silently from the room. He could see his brother was head over heels for the young doctor, and although he was happy for Rafa, he knew that his own actions would soon have terrible consequences for all of them.

Zani knew he shouldn't have returned from Europe; he should have stayed and faced the consequences of his behavior. No doubt if he had, he'd be dead.

But at least you won't have dragged Rafa, Bepi, your parents and that beautiful girl into your twisted mess of a life...

It was too late now. He'd made them all targets. Zani knew what his enemies would do to them—back in Europe, his own girlfriend, Sophia, had paid the price. He'd found her beaten and sobbing in their apartment upon returning from a club. Her attackers had left her a message to give Zani: Next time, she dies.

He used the last of his trust fund to make sure Sophie had safe haven in France; it was probably the only good thing he'd ever done in his wasteful life.

But now he was about to bring it all down on his family. His enemies had found him. He knew that because of one solitary text message: a photo sent to him.

Rafa and Noemi kissing in Rafa's car. So in love. The threat was clear.

Zani walked through the silent mansion. He could give himself up to his enemies, but it wouldn't do any good. They wanted revenge, and they would keep him alive just to watch his family die.

There was no hope. By his own actions, Zani had condemned the people he loved to death, and he knew that before they died, their lives would be made pure hell... and there was nothing he could do about it.

CHAPTER SIXTEEN

Rafa made good on his promise to take Noemi on vacation. He rented a private cabin on the shores of Lake Tahoe, and they flew into Carson City before renting a car and driving to the lake.

Rafa's parents had taken Depi for a few days, and so Noemi and Rafa were finally alone together. The cabin was small but private enough for the two of them to really enjoy each other.

The peace of the place was a balm on Noemi's grief, but it was Rafa who really saved her from the depths of despair. He kept her occupied the whole time, whether it was hiking around the lake or cooking meals together, and certainly at night, when they would sit out on the deck and make plans for their future. Noemi still hadn't told Rafa or anyone about the baby—she knew she couldn't ignore it forever but for the moment, she kept it to herself.

Their sex life became even more adventurous as they experimented with light BDSM. Noemi found she liked to have her hands bound behind her back as Rafa fucked her, liked being that helpless with him. The paddle she wasn't keen on, but the crop? Now that was a different, sweetly painful matter...

"You have dirty thoughts going on in that pretty head of yours,"

Rafa told her as they sat out on the deck, the remnants of their supper in front of them. Noemi picked up her glass of water—she was glad that he hadn't questioned why she didn't want wine—and sipped it, meeting his gaze.

"I was just thinking about that riding crop."

Rafa's smile widened. "That does it for you, doesn't it, baby?"

She nodded, her eyes sparkling with arousal. "When you're naked and stalking around me, your cock so thick and heavy, so hard and proud, huge against your belly, and you're wielding that crop... Jesus, Rafa..."

His hand slipped under her dress and into her panties and he grinned. "You're wet."

"Not as wet as I could be... I bet you could make me come just with that crop."

Rafa's lips crushed against hers. "Let's go test that theory."

SHE WAS in his arms and being carried to the bedroom. He dropped her onto the bed, and unbuttoned the simply cotton dress she wore, opening up the fabric, and trailing his lips down her bare skin. "I'm going to make you so wet, you're dripping," he said, his voice practically a growl, and Noemi wriggled with pleasure.

"First things, first." Rafa tied her hands behind her back, kissing her mouth, her jaw, her throat as he did. Laying her down, he stroked a finger down between her breasts then took each nipple into his mouth—just briefly—and then stood, stripping his own clothes off.

"Put the cock ring on," Noemi urged him, and Rafa chuckled.

"I'm not sure I'll need it looking at your beautiful body but if you like it..." He slid the metal cock ring to the base of his already stiffening cock.

"Perfect... you're perfect," Noemi breathed, and Rafa smiled. He picked up the short but heavy riding crop and slapped his palm with it.

"Where do you want this, baby?"

"Everywhere..." She gasped and arched her back as he brought the crop down hard across her belly. "God, yes... yes, Rafa."

He struck her breasts and her thighs as she squirmed with pleasure, he nudged her knees apart. "Spread those delicious thighs, baby, show me your cunt."

Noemi smiled as she drew her legs wide apart then squeaked as Rafa, grinning, brought the crop down across her sex, the tip catching her clit, making it jerk and pulse with pain and arousal. Her sex flooded, which didn't go unnoticed by Rafa.

"Juicy," he said with a lick of his lips, and sank to his knees.

"Uh-uh," Noemi sat up, shaking her head and laughing. "You made a deal. Make me come with the crop first then you can eat me all you want."

"Tyrant," he grumbled but stood and stalked around her, teasing her before bringing the crop down across her breasts. He whipped her until she was half-crying, half-laughing, and she came—hard.

So turned on was Rafa, that she was still mid-orgasm when he thrust his aching, diamond-hard cock into her, slamming his hips so hard against her that the bed moved. Noemi grinned up at him. "Fuck me hard, Genova..."

He obliged, reaching behind her to release her hands, and they immediately flew to his face, pulling his lips to hers hungrily. They moved together, completely uninhibited, their fingers bruising each other's skin in their mad desire for each other.

"What next?" A breathless Rafa grinned down at her as they recovered, and Noemi chuckled.

"Bend me over the breakfast bar," she said, her mind whirling with endorphins, "and fuck me in the ass."

"You sure?"

She nodded. "I've never tried it, and I want to do everything with you, Rafa."

"My pleasure."

Noemi gasped as he eased into her ass and moved gently. "Oh, God..."

Rafa's hand was stroking her clit, his lips were at her ear as he growled, "I'm going to make you cum so hard, baby."

And he did, Noemi's legs giving way as she screamed his name, her orgasm ripping through her. Rafa held her as they sank to the floor, panting for air and exhausted.

Noemi wound her body into his, her legs between his, her hands on his chest. "I love you so much, Rafa Genova. That was incredible."

"And just think, Doc, we've only just begun..."

Noemi giggled as he locked his arms around her and pulled her on top of him. She gazed down at his handsome face. The sadness she'd seen that had been almost always present was gone, and his gorgeous green eyes shone with love. He looked ten years younger: this man, her man.

"I've never felt this close to another person in my life," she said softly, "and it's not just the mind-blowing sex. It's you, Rafa."

Rafa smiled back at her. "It's us, Noe. We make sense; we always did. I'm going to tell you something now, something you may find... odd or strange."

"Go on."

Rafa stroked her hair back from her face. "Tomi... One afternoon, when we knew she was dying, after you'd had the accident and we didn't know if you'd make it, she told me something. It's been on my mind. She told me that if she could have picked the perfect partner for me, she would have picked you. She wished for it. She wished for us. Now, listen. As much as I adored Tomi, it's not the reason I'm with you, Noe. But she would have loved this. Us. She would have been so pleased that we found each other."

Noemi rolled off him and sat up, curling into a ball. Rafa sat up, not knowing whether she was upset and when he saw her shoulders shaking, he knew she was crying. "Hey."

He put his arm around her and she curled into him. "I'm sorry. That's so beautiful, Rafa..." She sniffled, trying to calm herself. "Rafa... I'm pregnant."

That he wasn't expecting. He drew in a deep breath. "Okay. Wow."

"I know. I swear, I am on birth control, but you know it's not always..." Noemi was rambling now, and Rafa, still reeling, realized he wasn't saying the right things, the things Noe needed to hear.

"Sweetheart, it's okay, I'm just a little..." He laughed. "We're having a baby?"

Noemi took a shaky breath in. "I'm pregnant... whether or not we have it is something we have to discuss."

Rafa felt ice in his veins. "You don't want it?"

"I don't know. I've been so mixed up since Jack died. I want to bear your children, Rafa, but the thought of having a child and losing it... it would kill me."

Rafa frowned. "Baby, we can't think like that. If we all thought like that, the human race would have died out millions of years ago."

Noemi nodded and Rafa could see how conflicted she was. "Look at me, baby."

She turned her lovely dark eyes on him, and he leaned his forehead against hers for a moment.

"I love you. Whatever you decide is right for you is fine with me. I'll just say this, and it's what I should have said first. God, I'm happy. A child with you is my dream, Noe. A whole family with you is my dream. Bepi would love a sibling. But we have time, all the time in the world, so if right now isn't going to work for you, then we take the next step. How far along are you?"

"About a month."

"So, we have time."

Noemi nodded and leaned her head onto his shoulder. "I want your babies, Rafa, I do. But we're just in the beginning part. We have Bepi to think of, your family, my family."

"Your career."

Noemi shook her head. "That's not... I'm a surgeon. They have kids all the time and go back to work. I wouldn't consider a baby a hindrance to my career." She chuckled suddenly. "I'm so mixed up, Rafa."

"Look, we don't have to make any decisions yet. Let's just enjoy these few days and when we get back to Seattle, we can talk more."

Noemi looked so relieved that Rafa smiled. She leaned against him. "I love you."

"I love you too, Nommy."

She smiled. "You should call Bepi. I bet he's driving your parents crazy." Her smile faded a little, and he noticed.

"What is it?"

"They're going to think I'm a gold digger."

Rafa gave a bark of laughter. "Believe me, they're not."

"But they know about us?"

"They do." It was his turn to hesitate. "At least, they know I'm seeing someone."

Noemi gaped at him. "But they don't know it's me?"

"Um..."

"Oh God."

Rafa shook his head. "Right now, I can't tell you why I haven't told them. I will, of course, as soon as we get back."

"At the same time, you can tell them I've trapped you with an unplanned pregnancy."

"Noe—"

"—that's how it's going to look." She got to her feet and padded away from him. For a moment, Rafa sat, shaking his head, then followed her into the bathroom.

Noemi was cranking on the shower.

"It's okay," she said sadly.

"No, it's not, and you're not being fair to them. They would never think that of you."

"But you didn't tell them. There must be a reason."

"I didn't tell them because you wanted to keep us secret!" The words came out harsher than he meant them to, but he also knew it was the truth. "It took Jack dying for you to tell your sister about us."

Noemi winced, and he regretted his words.

"Oh, wow," she said, her voice breaking, "that is so unfair."

"I'm sorry, That came out wrong. But you did want us on the down low."

"Because of this! First, I kill your fiancée, then I snag a billion-dollar donation for the hospital, and now I'm fucking you and carrying your child! How would that look to you?"

Rafa clenched his fists together and counted to ten. She was so screwed up. "Firstly, you did not kill Thomasina. I don't know how many times you need to be told that. Secondly, the donation was all about me trying to make sense of Thomasina's death and to show everyone that I, we, Bepi and me, we believed in you. Believe in you. Then we fell in love. To anyone else, that would seem a fairy tale, but to you..."

"Don't patronize me!" Noemi snapped, suddenly. "I'm not a child."

Rafa went very still. "Then stop behaving like one." He turned around and walked into the bedroom, grabbing his jeans and putting them on. He stalked out to the deck.

This couldn't go on. If Noemi couldn't get over her guilt about Thomasina, her perceived paranoia about what people would think of their relationship... how did they stand a chance?

He could hear the shower running from inside the cabin, running far too long. He guessed she was crying but maybe that's what she needed to do. She had lost so much, and Christ, the girl was only thirty years old. A baby. What she'd gone through...

He sat outside for an hour, trying to unravel his own thoughts. He heard the shower shut off and risked a quick glance through the large glass doors, but Noemi didn't appear in the living room. She needed some space. Good. Maybe they both did for a few minutes.

When the cool breeze from the lake made him shiver, he went inside. Noemi, in a white fluffy robe, her long dark hair damp from the shower. He went to her and took her face in his hands. Her eyes were red-rimmed and her cheeks puffy from crying. He kissed her gently, then nuzzled her nose with his. "I'm sorry I yelled."

Tears filled her eyes again, and she dashed them away impatiently. "I don't know what's wrong with me," she said, her voice gravelly, "I can't think straight."

Rafa wrapped his arms around her, but she didn't cry again. "Maybe it would help to talk to someone?"

He felt her nod. "Good. Then when we get back to Seattle, we'll arrange it."

"Okay."

He cupped her face with his hand. "Are you tired?"

She nodded, looking exhausted. "Come on, let's go to bed."

Rafa found himself falling asleep almost as soon as Noemi did, exhausted by everything that had happened. He fell into a deep, dreamless sleep, only to wake with a start in the deep blue moonlight as Noemi shook his awake.

Her eyes were huge and frightened as she put her finger to her lips. Rafa sat up, confused, and she leaned in to whisper in his ear.

"There's someone in the house."

CHAPTER SEVENTEEN

Noemi felt cold spikes of fear stabbing her body as Rafa told her to wait in the bedroom while he checked out the house. She had been awake, needing the bathroom, and when she was padding back to the bedroom, a shadow had passed the end of the hallway that led downstairs, and she almost shrieked with fright.

Instead she had clamped her hands over her mouth and listened. Had she imagined it? She reasoned it could have been something flying past one of the windows, causing a shadow from the bright moonlight, but then she heard a low voice, some barely audible cursing, and something shifting.

Now as she waited, she wished she had just yelled and scared the intruder off, instead of Rafa confronting who knows what. She stood at the door listening, her heart yammering away in her chest. She sneaked into the hallway, trying to see if he needed help—and a hand was clamped over her mouth.

Instantly her survival instinct kicked in, and she struggled with her captor, stomping on his instep. He released her with a roar, and Noemi screamed for Rafael.

"Noemi!" She heard his voice from downstairs followed by another sound as if he were being body slammed.

Noemi ran towards the stairs, but her attacker grabbed her again and threw her hard, down the shallow staircase. Noemi tumbled down, almost too shocked to feel the pain as her body crashed down the wooden stairwell.

She could hear sounds of fighting as she came to a stop, winded, but she didn't feel as if any limbs were broken. She heard her attacker walking down the stairs behind her, chuckling, and she tried to drag herself out of the stairway.

"Where are you going, pretty little thing? We ain't nearly done yet."

He hauled her up and carried her into the living room where Rafa was fighting with another man—and winning. Noemi screamed, and Rafa looked up just as the man threw Noemi at him. Rafa caught her and pushed her behind him.

"What the fuck do you want?" He yelled, and Noemi could see blood running down his face. Behind her was the breakfast bar. Surreptitiously, she reached behind her, her hand groping for anything they could use as a weapon. There was a flash of light, and she realized the attackers were taking photos on their phone. Rafa lunged at them, but Noemi pulled him back. He was a strong man but against two of them...

Noemi's attacker smirked and nodded to his accomplice, and they went out the same way they came in—through the unlocked sliding doors that led to the deck. Rafa cussed loudly, and then went to the doors, locking them. Rafa and Noemi stood in shocked silence for a long time before Rafa came to her. "Are you okay?"

She nodded and touched his face. "But you're not."

"I'm fine. I'm going to call the police. Then afterward, we're getting out of here. If I were alone, I'd say fuck it, but I'm not risking the two of you." He splayed his hand over her belly and at that moment, Noemi knew she would keep the baby.

The police came, and they gave a statement, but the police told them it was probably an attempted robbery, and that they would keep a look out. Noemi read that as 'they're long gone, forget about it.' She could see Rafa wasn't happy with that answer, but he didn't press it.

As soon as the officers left, he turned to her, his green eyes full of fury and concern. "Sweetheart, let's get out of here."

Noemi obeyed him, and within a half hour they were on the road.

THEY CHECKED into a hotel in Carson City, but Rafa insisted they fly back to Seattle as soon as they had gotten some sleep. "I want you far, far away from here."

She cleaned up his head wound, which looked much worse than it was, and he tried to persuade her to see a doctor, but Noemi knew she was okay. "I'll probably just ache tomorrow. I was lucky; those stairs weren't too steep."

"We were both lucky. I just want to know who the fuck those guys were."

Noemi dabbed at his forehead with the rubbing alcohol, and he winced. "Like the cops said, probably just opportunists."

"Opportunists don't throw pregnant women down stairs. Opportunists steal. They took nothing but photographs of us."

Noemi gave him a half-smile. "He didn't know I was pregnant, baby."

They gazed at each other for a long moment, then both began to smile. "We're really going to do this, huh?" Rafa said, his eyes shining, and Noemi laughed.

"I guess we are."

He kissed her softly. "I love you."

"Right back at you, big guy." She sighed and laid her head against his shoulder. "I'd show you how much, but I really am wiped out."

They laid down together, and Rafa tucked his arms around her waist as they fell asleep. As she gave into unconsciousness, Noemi knew that when they woke up, they would have to plan for a very different future than either of them had expected.

· · ·

ZANI FLICKED through the images on the text message he'd just been sent. Rafa. Noemi. These bastards had followed them to the cabin, attacked them, taken photos of them. It was a warning. Had they said anything to Rafa, given him a clue that it was Zani's fault they were attacked? He felt sick. Were his brother and his lover hurt?

Jesus...

No. They couldn't have told Rafa anything, or he would have been on the phone asking Zani what the fuck he'd gotten himself into in Europe. Zani closed his eyes. He'd been more than just reckless. His love for cocaine had led to his owing money to men who didn't give credit... ever. Zani had thought he was untouchable. Now he knew he wasn't, and neither were the people he loved.

And he had no idea how to save them.

CHAPTER EIGHTEEN

Noemi and Rafa decided not to tell anyone about the baby until past the three-month mark. "That'll give Leo some time to come to terms, and anyway, it's traditional."

Rafa grinned at his lover as they sat in his kitchen one morning a week after their return from Lake Tahoe. "Like any of this has been traditional."

Noemi chuckled and linked her fingers in his. "Then a little bit of tradition is probably called for." She rubbed her belly unconsciously. "I should go get it confirmed at the hospital, though. They'd keep it on the down low—they'd have to—and, don't freak out—but I want to just check everything is okay."

Rafa was immediately alert. "You've had pain?"

"A little but that's not unusual, so don't get panicked," She waved him down as he began to rise from his chair. "After all, my body is changing. I'm still waiting for the morning sickness to kick in." She leaned over and brushed her lips against his. "Sure you'll still want me when I'm all fat and huge?"

"Even more, Fatty."

She laughed out loud. "So cruel, but I love you."

"I'm gonna spoil you, pretty girl. Anything you want: pickled ice cream at midnight, scrambled eggs and surströmming at three a.m."

"What the hell is surströmming?" Noemi was giggling at the mischief on his face.

"Fermented herring. Smells like death."

Noemi gagged, and Rafa grinned. "Still waiting for the morning sickness?"

"I hate you."

He blew her a kiss, and she laughed as Zani came into the room. "Hey, Zani."

"Hey, Noe, Rafa. Everyone good?"

"Of course." Rafa looked at his brother. "So, I'm going into the office this morning. Want to come with and discuss what use we can put you to?"

Zani smiled thinly. "Whatever you say, brother. I'll go get changed."

He slunk from the room and Rafa frowned. "You think he's acting strangely? I mean ever since we got back?"

Noemi shrugged. "I don't know him well enough to know, baby. What do you think?"

Rafa sighed. "I don't know... I guess I could talk to him today."

"You think he really wants a job?"

Rafa shook his head, smiling ruefully. "No, but what can I do?" He kissed her. "I'm going to get Bepi up."

"I can take him to the kindergarten if you like."

"I bet he'd love that—" Rafa was walking towards the door, then stopped and returned to her. "And maybe while you're doing that... you could think about moving in with me."

Noemi's eye widened. "Wow. Wow. I mean... wow."

"Just think about it is all I ask. I would very much like to raise our child together, but if that's too soon..."

Noemi chuckled. "I think we've thrown 'too soon' out of the window."

"Is that a yes?"

Noemi grinned. "Yes, you beautiful man, I'll move in with you. But, one condition."

"Back rubs and dirty sex nightly?"

Noemi pretended to look affronted. "I would hope that was a given. No, my condition is I pay rent. I'm not freewheeling from you, Rafa. No way. And it's not like I can't afford it, I'm a surgeon for Chrissakes. So... whatever your mortgage payment is on this every month, I pay half."

Rafa's lips twitched. "You want to know how much my mortgage is per month?"

"Yes."

He told her, and Noemi paled. "Well... how about I just rent a room?"

Rafa threw his head back and laughed. "Girl, listen. Money is just... stuff. Who cares? We'll work it out! No one will think you're a gold digger! You're a surgeon, remember?"

"Gah. Trapped by my own words."

"Yup." Rafa batted her butt with his hand. "Come shower with me, and I'll take my rent that way."

"Perv."

"You know it."

Bepi was, of course, delighted to be taken to the kindergarten by 'Nommy,' and he chatted all the way. He hugged her tightly when she said goodbye. "Love you, Nommy."

Noemi held her tears back, and she smiled. "Love you, too, Bepi."

She was still thinking about him as she drove to see Leonora. If she, Noemi, could love Bepi this fiercely when she wasn't even his mother, she could not even comprehend how Leo was dealing with the loss of Jack. The pain must be overwhelming, she thought, and the idea of Leo suffering made her press the gas pedal a little more.

Noemi let herself into her sister's house, calling out to Leo as she did. There was no answer, and Noemi felt a little curl of fear in her stomach. "Leo?"

"I'm out in the yard."

Relief flooded through her, and she followed the sound of her sister's voice into the small yard. She saw Leo crouched on the grass, digging around the bottom of a small tree.

"Hey," she looked around at Noemi, and Noemi was relieved that Leo looked a little better.

"That's lovely," she nodded at the tree, and Leo smiled.

"It's a gift from Jack's school. They've planted another in their field from the same sapling in his honor. Honey, are you crying?"

Noemi wiped her eyes. "Sorry, so emotional lately."

Leo stood, smacking her hands together to get rid of the mud. "Jeez, you're not pregnant, are you?"

Noemi was relived Leo didn't seem to need an answer. "How are you?"

"Same as I was when you asked me yesterday, boo." Leonora's smile was too bright, and Noemi could tell her sister's temper was on the edge.

"Fair enough," she said lightly, not wanting a row. "Just wondered if you'd like to come and walk Mouse with me. We're going out to Alki Beach Park."

"No, thanks. I'm meeting some friends in the city later."

"Oh, okay." Noemi was a little stung by Leo's brusque dismissal. "Leo...? Is ever—"

"Noe, I swear, if you ask me if everything is okay one more time..."

"Fine, fine. I get the message." Noemi said it softly, but she could feel the tears coming again. She turned away. "Well, call me when you want to get together."

"I will. Later."

Noemi nodded, not looking at her sister. "Later."

SHE DROVE out to Alki Beach and let Mouse out to run, envying the dog's boundless joy as she ran free. Oh, to have such an uncomplicated life, she thought fondly. The day was sunny, but a cold breeze blew up from Elliott Bay, and she shivered, pulling her thin denim jacket around her. She walked for an hour, playing with Mouse on the grassy lawns. There were a few people around also walking their dogs, but after an hour, she noticed she was alone apart from a solitary man, walking a few meters behind her.

She didn't pay any attention to him until Mouse skittered up to her and growled, staring behind her, her hackles up. Noemi stopped and turned, glancing behind her. The man had stopped when she had.

Fuck. Annoyed rather than scared, Noemi clipped Mouse's leash back on and walked towards the man. She kept eye contact with him until she had passed him, a silent warning—I will fight back, asshole, and so will my dog. Mouse jerked slightly at her leash, snarling towards the man, but he did not flinch, just smirked.

Noemi stopped suddenly and took out her phone. Openly, deliberately, she took a photo of the man. "Just so you know, that's gone to the Cloud," she said to him. "So, anything happens to me or my dog between now and my car... they'll know your face."

"Hey, I'm just walking here." His grin was mocking and surly. He made a lewd gesture towards his crotch, and Noemi gave him the finger.

"Right... men like you make me sick. You think we don't feel you standing too close or watching us like predators? Creep. Go back to your momma's basement, you fucking loser."

"Man, you're one stuck-up bitch." His grin had vanished. Mouse growled. The man glared at Noemi and stalked off. Noemi smiled grimly. Asshole. She looked down at Mouse.

"We showed him, Mousie." Mouse licked her hand, and Noemi bent to kiss her dog's furry head. "Glad you're here though."

She walked back to the car, and despite her bravado, locked herself and Mouse in as she drove to the hospital. She opened the backdoor of the car and put Mouse in the lockable dog cage, making sure she had enough water and fussing over her. "I won't be too long, bubba."

. . .

SHE SNUCK up to Gynecology and found her friend Joan, the head nurse. She told her news and asked her if she would scan her. "Just to be sure. I took a fall the other day, and I just want to check."

Joan grinned at her, obviously delighted for her. "Of course. I warn you though, if it's only a month or so, then all we'll see is the gestational sac, so don't ask me what sex he or she is."

Noemi grinned. "I won't. Can we do a pregnancy test too? I mean I took a bunch, but it never seems official until it's done by the hospital."

Joan rolled her eyes. "You nerd. Fine, come with me. I assume you're not telling anyone yet?"

"Not yet."

A few minutes later, Joan smiled at her. "Well, you're definitely preggo. Let's see what we can see on this sucker."

She squirted cold gel on Noemi's belly and started the scan. "Well, sweetie, you're about six weeks, a little more than you thought."

Noemi was surprised but nodded. "Not impossible."

Joan grinned at her. "Planned?"

"Not exactly but wanted."

Joan was grinning mischievously. "Really? Both of them?"

Noemi's eyes widened. "What?"

Joan moved the screen around. "Congrats Momma... you're having twins."

Noemi burst into tears, half-laughing, half-crying. "Oh, my God... twins? Really?"

"Really. One. Two." She pointed out the tiny embryos. "Good news?"

Noemi nodded, unable to speak. Joan hugged her then cleaned her up. "I'll give you a moment."

"Thanks, Joanie."

When she was alone, Noemi took out her phone and called Rafa. She got his voicemail but didn't want to tell him on a message. "Sweetie, I know you're working, but I'm coming over. I have some news. Some very good news."

. . .

SHE WENT BACK DOWN to the parking lot, unlocked Mouse's cage, and got the dog out to walk her around. Mouse was delighted to see her as if she hadn't seen her for days rather than forty-five minutes. Noemi walked her around until the dog peed, then loaded her back up and drove into the city. She knew Rafa wouldn't mind if Mouse came into his office with her, and so she got out, clicked on the leash and started to walk to the elevator.

The skin on the back of her neck prickled, and she turned, scanning the parking lot. The feeling of being watched was back—but she knew that was ridiculous. The guy in the park, the intruders at Lake Tahoe... why on earth would any of them be here? Mouse didn't seem to be upset at all.

Man, pregnancy hormones are making me crazy, she told herself as she walked to the elevator.

As she rode up, Mouse sitting patiently next to her, Noemi put a hand on her belly. Twins. She could barely believe it. She was still smiling when she said hello to Rafa's assistant Mary.

"You can go in; they're just chatting."

Noemi thanked her but still knocked. Rafa stood and came to meet her. "Hey, beautiful."

Zani looked relieved at the interruption—he got up and kissed her cheek. "Savior," he muttered and disappeared out of the room. Noemi chuckled as Rafa closed the door, giving them some privacy. He mussed Mouse's fur and grinned at Noemi.

"This is a lovely surprise."

Noemi beamed at him. "I hope I'm about to give you another. I went to the hospital and had a scan. I'm definitely pregnant; all is doing well... and by all, I mean..." She grinned as she built it up. "... both of them are doing fine."

"Twins?" Rafa's eyes widened, and he laughed. "We're having twins?"

"Ssh," Noemi said, nodding to the closed office door as his voice got louder, but then she shrieked with laughter as Rafa picked her up and swung her around.

He set her down on her feet and took her face in his hands. "You have made me so happy, Noemi Castor. So very happy."

"As have you, my darling." She tangled her fingers in his dark curls. "I love you."

Rafa kissed her, then splayed his hand over her belly. "Two of them," he said, his tone incredulous.

"I'm about six weeks," she said. "Can you believe it?"

He kissed her again, his lips pressed hard against hers. "I can't believe how lucky I am."

Rafa asked her to sit with him for a time, and they talked excitedly about their children. Then Noemi grinned. "Zani looked drained. You been driving him hard?"

Rafa rolled his eyes. "If you asked him that, he would definitely say yes. To anyone not spoiled? He got off easy."

Noemi laughed. "Poor little rich boy."

"Indeed." Rafa sighed. "Thing is... he's not untalented. He could really make an impact. He's much more sociable than me. His natural charm? He could charm snakes from trees."

"You're pretty charming yourself, Mr. Genova."

Rafa grinned and kissed her. "You're the only person I want to charm."

"Done and done." She laid her head on his shoulder, feeling tired. It had been a weird morning. "Listen, I'll leave you in peace."

Rafa kissed her temple. "You don't have to go."

"I should." She smiled at him. "After all, I've got to go pack some stuff, bring it over, you know. Can you spare a drawer?"

Rafa laughed. "Every drawer. You just take all the space you need. Listen, you need anything, just charge it to my credit card."

"Nuh-uh." She wagged her finger at him, and he chuckled.

"Fine. But look, I want it to be our home, so you want to change anything? Go right ahead, rip out walls, paint it neon pink, anything."

"I'm tempted to paint it neon pink just because now," Noemi giggled. "You madman. Look, we can nest all we want later." She kissed him and got up. For a second, she was tempted to tell him about the creep in the park, but then why upset him? Her news had put him in such a good mood, and it wasn't like she'd ever see the guy again—with any luck.

"Hey, listen, I overheard Mary talking about this great baby store in the city once."

"Honeybees, I know. Leo went there when Jack was born." Noemi swallowed over a sudden lump, and Rafa noticed. He put his arms around her.

"I'm sorry, honey."

She shook her head. "No need. I saw Leo this morning. She seems to be... coping. Maybe a little too well. I'm glad I have this time off work because I think, whether she likes it or not, I should keep an eye on her." She chewed her lips "The twins..."

Rafa nodded at her hesitation. "We don't have to tell anyone yet, baby. We'll work it out."

NOEMI TOOK Mouse into the city and found the baby clothing store. She was about to tie Mouse up outside when the owner waved her in. "There's no one here; bring her in."

The owner was clearly a dog lover. She fussed over Mouse while Noemi looked around and chatted to her. Noemi bought a few things and thanked her.

She walked slowly back to the parking garage, and she was already sitting in the car before she saw the photograph stuck to her windshield. A Polaroid? She didn't even think they made those anymore. She got out and plucked it from under the wiper blade.

A shiver went through her. The photograph was of her, chatting to the woman in the baby store. Less than a half hour ago. "Jesus Christ..." she whispered. She got back into the car and banged the locks down, looking around. She couldn't see anyone else in the garage, and she started the car and drove out as quickly as possible.

But now she knew. It wasn't her hormones making her paranoid.

Someone was watching her.

CHAPTER NINETEEN

In her apartment, she packed a few things quickly, hoping Mouse would alert her to any intruders, but feeling the anxiety from being stalked anyway. She threw some clothes into a bag feeling like a candy-ass, but the photograph had rattled her. Put together with the attack in Tahoe and the man in the park this morning...

Why would anyone be stalking her?

She jumped as her cell phone rang. "Hello?"

"Noemi? Drew Ballentine."

Noemi blinked, her mind going blank for a second. "Oh. Sorry. Hi, how are you?"

"I'm good, thank you. I just wanted to check in with you after our chat the other day. Kit said you might need someone to talk to, especially after the terrible tragedy. How is your family?"

Noemi felt an irrational irritation but pushed it aside. It was nice of him to call, to care, but she didn't know the man. "We're coping as best we can. Listen, Drew, it's sweet of you to call, but it's not a great time for me to talk. I'm sorry."

"That's okay, dear."

Noemi nearly laughed. Dear? The guy was only a few years older than her. Dear? "Some other time?"

"I'll hold you to that, Noemi. For now, take care."

"You too."

She hung up and dropped her phone on her bed, shaking her head. So, Kit had decided she needed to talk to a minister of all people? Her, an atheist, something Kit knew very well. She felt irritable, argumentative again, and had to talk herself out of calling Kit and yelling at him for his presumption. She knew he meant well, that he cared, but it was galling. Why did everybody else think they knew what was best for her all the time?

Her phone bleeped again, and she gave a small growl of irritation. Her stomach dropped when she saw the message. Another photograph of her, this time walking into the hospital. Noemi stared at it. Could it be a coincidence that Drew Ballentine had called her right before? Was he sending her a message?

Was it possible that he knew about her and Rafa, that he was angry she had begun a relationship with his stepsister's lover?

Noemi closed her eyes, trying to quell the panic inside. No. Kit, her good friend Kit, was a good judge of character—if he suspected Drew's motives were less than noble, he would never have encouraged it. She dialed his number.

"Hey, cutie tootie," came his voice, and Noemi relaxed.

"Hey, KitKat. Listen, no biggie, but did you ask Drew Ballentine to talk to me? Counsel me?"

"Um," Kit sounded guilty, and instantly she knew he had. "Yeah, I did. I was worried, sweetie, that's all, and Drew's a good guy. I know you're not religious, but Drew seems like a good person to help you, is all. Sorry if that was overstepping."

Noemi smiled down the phone, relieved. "It's okay. I mean, it is overstepping a little, but I'll take it from you. After everything we've done together, seen together, I'll take it from you."

"It came from a good place, I swear."

"I know." Noemi hesitated. "You sure Drew is on the regular?"

Kit chuckled. "Pretty sure."

"Kit... I'm seeing Rafael Genova."

Kit was silent. "Ah."

"So, you can see where I'd be hesitant about confiding in Drew."

"I do. Ah, damn, girl, I'm sorry. That'll teach me to interfere. Hey, good news though. Does he make you happy?"

Noemi put her hand on her belly, thinking of her twins. "Unbelievably so."

"I'm glad. Listen... do you want me to talk to Drew or..."

"No, I'll meet him, explain the situation. He may feel like it would be a conflict of interest, but I owe him a coffee and an explanation at the very least."

"Good on you, sweetie."

NOEMI CALLED Drew Ballentine back and arrange to meet him the next day. "I think there's something you ought to know, Drew."

"I will look forward to seeing you, Noemi."

RAFA SAT BACK in his chair, his good mood from earlier gone. "Zani... I'm trying here. But if you're just going to crap on every suggestion I have..."

Zani shifted uncomfortably in his chair. "Well, if you weren't quite so patronizing..."

"Grow up." Rafa had had enough and snapped at his brother. "You think I got where I am by just trading on the fact I'm Dad's son? No. It took hard work to convince the Board of Trustees and our partners that I knew what I was talking about. I've grown the business every year since I took over, and it was damn hard work." He gazed at his brother, his eyes cold. "Even when Tomi was sick, I still worked while you were partying around Europe, shoving God knows what up your nose, and sticking your dick into everything."

Zani got up. "Yeah well, that's going to change now."

"Why? You run out of money?" Rafa already knew the answer to that and knew it was cruel to ask, but Zani had gotten on his last nerve this morning. Zani wanted to start at the top of the pile, not put in the work that Rafa had. Zani wanted everything handed to him on a silver platter.

Not going to happen. Rafa sighed and threw his pen down on the desk. "Look, Zani, you know my thoughts. You're not without talent—you could be invaluable, especially when it comes to schmoozing the clients. But that would mean travelling a lot back to Europe. You seem to not want to make an effort to do that."

"It's not that I—" Zani broke off. He stared out of the window. "I can't go back, is all."

"Why? Why not?"

Zani just shook his head, and Rafa had finally had enough. "We're not getting anywhere," he said, "and I have actual work to do. I'll see you at home later, Zani."

Rafa was glad Zani left without arguing, but he couldn't shake the irritation he felt. Zani's behavior was nothing short of a spoiled rich boy, and that wasn't going to fly anymore.

Rafa sighed and rubbed his eyes, feeling a little overwhelmed by life. About to be a father of twins by his dead lover's doctor? Did he really have the right to judge Zani on his willful behavior? No. Totally different situation, he told himself. He loved Noemi and was over-joyed about the babies. Bepi, too, would love siblings.

There was one thing he still had to do, however, and he picked up the telephone now. "Mom? Hey, Mom, how are you? Good. Listen... I have something to tell you and Dad and it's pretty, well...big. Life changing. I don't suppose you and Dad are free for dinner later this week, are you? Good, I'll book a restaurant—and Mom? I'm bringing someone with me. I'll tell you more later..."

NOEMI HAD ALSO DECIDED to go visit her parents and talk to them. She needed to tell someone about the pregnancy, and when she got to her parents' house and found her mother alone, she was relieved. Marian, always the gracious host, fussed around her adoptive daughter as Noemi sat, plucking up the courage to tell her the news.

"Mom?"

Marian Castor smiled at her daughter. "Yes, sweetie?"

"I'm pregnant."

Marian sat down with a thump, shocked. For a second, she couldn't speak, and Noemi waited, her heart thumping. Finally, Marian took her hand. "You can't tell Leo. Not yet."

"I know." Even though Noemi had been expecting that answer, she was still filled with dismay. "Mom... it's twins."

Despite her shock, Marian beamed. "Oh, how wonderful, Noe. I'm assuming Rafael...?"

Noemi nodded. "Good," Marian said approvingly, "he's a good man."

They sat in silence for a few moments, Marian stroking her daughter's hand. Noe looked at her mother. "Do you think she'll ever be ready to hear about the twins?"

Marian sighed. "Sweetheart... how do you get over something like that? Jack? He was her everything." She squeezed Noemi's hand. "I've never told you this, but the year before we adopted you, I had a miscarriage. A late one, almost full term. It was a girl, and I had to give birth to her. We held her for hours before they took her away. She was so perfect; we could hardly believe she wasn't just sleeping."

"Oh, Momma, I'm so sorry." Noemi's eyes filled with tears. "Why didn't you ever tell me?"

"We didn't tell either of you. Leo was too young to understand. I don't even think she remembers I was pregnant, to be honest. We didn't explain things to children the way they do now. We just told Leo she was getting a baby sister. And she did. God, Noe, the moment they told us you were ours..."

Noemi burst into tears, and her mother wrapped her arms around her. "Momma, I'm so lucky to have you as parents. So, so lucky. I wish I could do something to help ease the pain for all of you. I can't bear it.... Poor Jack. Poor Leo."

Marian's eyes were wet, too, as she released Noemi. "I know. Listen... she'll obviously have to be told when you start to show. Until then, how about we keep it our secret?"

. . .

NOEMI WAS NAPPING when Rafa got home, and she stirred as he pulled off his tie, kicked off his shoes and lay down beside her, tucking his arm around her waist.

"Hey, handsome."

"Hey, pretty girl. Go back to sleep."

Noemi shook her head. "No, my head is groggy. Wake me up, Rafa."

He smiled and kissed her. "My pleasure." He moved to cover her body with his, parting the robe she was wearing and kissing her throat, moving down to her breasts as she stroked his curls.

When his lips reached her belly, he suddenly blew a raspberry on her skin, and Noemi burst out laughing, the sudden release of tension welcome. Rafa grinned up at her. "Hey, you think they can hear me if I talk to them?"

"I don't think they have ears yet, baby." Noemi chuckled then sighed happily as his tongue traced a circle around her navel. His fingers hooked into her panties and drew them down her legs, and he hooked her knees over his shoulders.

He nipped gently at her clit with his teeth before lashing his tongue around it, teasing it until it was rock-hard and ultra-sensitive, and Noemi was writhing beneath his touch, giving herself over completely.

Rafa's tongue dipped deep into her sodden wet cunt, and Noemi cried out. His thumb began to stroke her clit as his tongue slid along her slit and down inside her, and she felt a wave of unstoppable pleasure as she came, shivering and breathless.

She couldn't wait any longer and demanded that he strip, freeing his demanding cock from his underwear and guiding him inside her. She lived for these moments, their bodies entwined, so close, so intimate. Rafa smiled down at her as they made love, his green eyes shining, so full of love, that she forgot anything else existed and just concentrated on him, her love.

. . .

AFTERWARDS, they showered together and went to the kitchen to find something to eat. Bepi, already in bed when Rafa got home, began to cry—a childish nightmare—and they sat with him, reading to him until he fell asleep again. Rafa kissed his son's forehead and smiled up at Noemi. "See," he whispered, "you're already a Momma."

They were walking back to their bedroom when they heard the commotion at the front door. Rafa sighed. "It's Zani. Go to bed, sweetheart. Let me deal with this."

NOEMI WAITED for him in the bedroom, and when he returned, she saw his face was grim. "He's drunk and possibly high. Who the fuck knows? I put him in a cab and sent him to a hotel. No way is he staying here in that condition, not with you and Bepi in the house."

Noemi held out her arms, and he went into them. "I swear to God," he said, his voice muffled as he buried his face in her hair, "if I never saw him again..."

"Don't say that," she said gently. "Look, he's obviously an addict. How about I talk to him, try to get him into rehab?"

"No." Rafa looked up at her, his eyes cold. "Let him take responsibility for once. He needs to hit rock bottom before he can see it for himself."

But what Rafa didn't know was that when Zani hit rock bottom... he would take them with him.

CHAPTER TWENTY

Noemi walked into the coffee shop on Fifth and saw Drew Ballentine waiting for her. He stood up and shook her hand. "Coffee?"

"Decaf, please."

He was dressed more casually than last time, a vintage T-shirt and jeans—expensive designer jeans, but still, it was less 'car salesman' than when she first met him.

"I'm glad you decided to do this," he said when he returned with her coffee. "Although I don't want you to feel as if—"

"Drew, I'm having a sexual and romantic relationship with Rafael Genova."

Rip off the Band-Aid. She watched the emotions on his face: surprise, shock, unease. Then he sighed and nodded. "Thank you for telling me."

She couldn't figure out how he felt. "I assure you, it only began recently, and had nothing, nothing to do with my relationship with Thomasina. I adored her; she was my patient but also my friend."

Drew nodded, but the look in his eyes was less than warm. "I see."

"I'm telling you this now because it was only fair that you know before you offer me any... counseling. I thank you for the offer, but I really don't think it would be appropriate." She tried to smile at him. "But I would like us to be friends, if that's something you could consider? We have a common link in Bepi."

Drew nodded. "We do, that's obvious. Look, again, thank you for telling me. I think you're right, I'm probably not best placed to advise you."

"Look," Noemi said. "I'm a big girl. If I feel I need counseling, I'll seek it. I know how these things work. I know both you and Kit meant well, but I'm an adult. I have my family, my loved ones."

"Are you in love with Rafael?"

She nodded, meeting his gaze steadily. "Very much so." She gave him a half-smile. "If your next sentence is something like 'then you should know the truth about him,' I warn you, I'll take it with a grain of salt."

Drew laughed. "There is something you should know about Rafa: he made my sister very happy. He's a terrific father and a good man."

Noemi smiled at him. "Thank you."

"As for the other thing, you'll have to forgive my presumption. To be honest with you, since Tomi's death, I've been struggling. I should have been here more, should have spent more time with her. I regret that."

"Then spend more time with Bepi now. I'm sure he'd love to know his uncle."

Drew smiled at her gratefully. "I will, thank you."

Noemi went to the hospital afterwards and told Lazlo she wanted to come back to work. "It's time, Laz, time to get back on the horse."

"I'm glad, Noe. We could do with your help around here. Finn resigned."

Noemi was shocked. "Oh, no..."

Lazlo nodded, his expression unhappy. "He's not dealing with Jack's death well."

"It wasn't his fault."

Lazlo smiled at her kindly. "I remember saying something similar to you many, many times. Finn, like you, will believe that when he believes that."

"I guess." Noemi shook her head. "Ever wonder if it's worth it? This career? For the loss?"

They looked at each other and then smiled. "Yes," they said in unison.

"Although, I should tell you, Laz... I'm going to need some time off in about seven and a half months." Noemi was nervous now, but Lazlo laughed.

"Oh, sweetheart, congratulations! I take it you're not telling anyone yet?"

"Not yet. Obviously, Laz, if you do see Leo... we haven't told her yet so..."

"Gotcha." He got up and hugged her. "I hope you and Rafael are very happy."

"Thank you, Laz."

NOEMI WENT BACK to Rafa's mansion, feeling more settled than she had for a while. One thing at a time, she thought now. She dumped her purse on the bed, but it fell off and the Polaroid photograph that had been left on her windshield fell out. She picked it up, studying it. She hadn't told Rafa about it or the one sent to her phone, distracted by other things but now she felt foolish. It was weird, right?

She put it back in her purse and resolved to talk to Rafa about it when he got home. She drove to collect Bepi from kindergarten, singing and chatting with him as they went home. She served him milk and cookies as they sat in the kitchen.

"Nommy?"

"Yes, bubba?"

He looked at her with wide green eyes, so like his father's. "Do you remember my mommy?"

Noemi felt her heart ache. "I do, sweetie, very well. Your mommy was so lovely. She was funny and kind and she loved you more than anything."

"More than Pa?"

Noemi smiled. "It's a different kind of love. You'll understand when you grow up. But she loved you both with all her heart."

Bepi was silent for a long moment, drinking his milk. Then he put his glass down. "I can't remember her much anymore," he said, his little face ashamed, and Noemi hugged him, pulling him onto her lap. "It's not nice to not remember Mommy."

"Darling, you were very, very young when Mommy died. It's not your fault; this is what happens. In a strange way, it happens so that you can feel less sad. I promise, Pa and me, we won't let you forget her. Not ever. Okay?"

Bepi nodded and snuggled into her as she held him. They stayed there for a while, just hugging until there was a large crash, and they both jumped out of their skins.

Shocked, Bepi started to wail, and Noemi tried to comfort him. "It's okay, baby."

She heard Zani laugh from the foyer, and her face set with anger. "Whoops!" Zani cackled as he almost fell into the kitchen. He grinned widely at them both, and Noemi felt her heart sink. From his pinpoint pupils to the strong whiff of alcohol emanating from him, Zani was out of control, and Noemi didn't want Bepi to see his uncle like that.

She got up, clutching the little boy. "Zani, grab yourself some coffee and stay here."

"I smashed a bottle out there." He waved in the general direction of the hallway.

"I'll clean it up. Just let me settle Bepi." She hurried Bepi, who had gone very quiet, up to his bedroom. "Sweetie, just stay up here for a while. I'll come and see to you when Pa gets home."

Bepi's eyes were wide. "Is Uncle Zani okay?"

"He is, darling. He's just tired." She kissed Bepi's forehead and went back down stairs. She saw the bottle of champagne smashed on the marble floor and gritted her teeth. Rafa would go insane that his security let Zani into the house in that condition.

She picked up the biggest pieces of glass then went back into the kitchen to find something to clean up the alcohol and small pieces.

Zani was standing, facing away from her, bent over the counter. Noemi couldn't believe it, but he was snorting up a line of white powder.

"What the fuck do you think you're doing?" She was yelling, but she didn't care. She dumped the broken glass in the trash and pushed him away from the counter. Remnants of white powder were stuck to the granite as well as around the edge of Zani's nostrils.

He laughed, then his eyes flared with desire as he looked at her. "God, I have to give it to my brother... you really are a gorgeous woman."

He lurched at her, but she sidestepped him, and he fell against the counter. "Aww, come on, Noe, gimme some sugar."

Was this guy for real?

"I think you've had far too much sugar, Zani. Rafa will be home soon. You want him to see you like this?"

She moved to grab a cloth to clean up the countertop, but he grabbed her around the waist and swung her around. "Dance with me."

"No... let me go!"

Noemi struggled with him, but Zani was a big man, strong like Rafa, and with cocaine pumping through his system, her slight frame was no match. He grabbed her hand and 'danced' her around the room, quicker and quicker until she felt sick.

"Zani, let me go now, please." She pleaded with him, but he just laughed. He moved faster as she tried to free herself, but then Zani stumbled and they both fell, Zani's weight on top of Noemi. She felt her back smash into the cold tile of the floor, Zani's elbow in her solar plexus.

Winded, she choked as she saw Rafa's furious face from behind Zani's prone body. He hauled his brother off of her and threw him across the room before scooping her up. "What the hell is going on?"

Noemi caught her breath, opened her mouth to speak, but then saw Zani convulsing, frothing at the mouth. Fuck.

"Rafa, call 911." She darted to his brother, shifting him onto his side, making sure his airways were clear. Zani's eyes were open and staring.

"What the hell?"

"He's overdosing, I think. Zani? Zani, if you can hear me, squeeze my hand." Noemi waited as she held Zani's hand but felt nothing. "Shit. Rafa, get the paramedics here. I'm going to try to help him breathe."

She blew air into Zani's lungs, feeling for a pulse. It was there but weak. She would have to keep him breathing until the paramedics arrived.

"Pa?"

Oh no. Noemi looked up to see Bepi, his little face terrified. Rafa, talking to the paramedics, picked his son up and hugged him.

"It's okay, slugger. Zani's not feeling well is all."

"Take him out of here," Noemi said softly, "because I can't be sure..."

She didn't have to say the words. I can't be sure Zani won't die.

Rafa nodded and went out of the room. Noemi kept up her efforts until the paramedics arrived and relinquished her control gratefully as the first responders treated Zani.

Zani gave a cough, and with a painful gasp, regained consciousness and flailed around. "Zani, listen, it's me, Noemi. Just relax."

She made the mistake of stepping too close, and he lashed out, his closed fist connecting with her cheek. She staggered back as one of the paramedics caught her. "I'm okay," she said.

"They do that," the paramedic said sympathetically, steadying her. "We'll put restraints on him before we take him to the hospital. You okay?"

Noemi nodded. Rafa came back and put his arms around her as they loaded Zani into the ambulance. "We'll follow you," he told the paramedics. "Are you okay, baby?"

Noemi nodded, shaken but calm. "I'm good. Listen, let's get Bepi and—"

She tailed off as she saw a car approaching the house. Leo's car. What was her sister doing here?

Leonora got out, his eyes full of concern. "I just saw an ambulance... is everything okay?"

Rafa explained and Leo nodded. "Why don't I come with you? I can look after Bepi while you're with Zani."

Noemi was surprised and while Rafa was getting Bepi, she turned to her sister. "Why were you coming by?"

"I was rude to you, and I wanted to apologize. I'm happy you've found love, Noe, I really am. Rafael's a good man."

Noemi smiled at her sister. "That's a popular opinion. Come on, let's go."

THEY DROVE INTO THE CITY, and Leo took Bepi to the Relative's Room while Rafa and Noemi went to see Zani. To their great relief, he was conscious—rambling—but conscious. He reached out his hand when he saw them. "Rafa... Noe... I fucked up. I'm so sorry. So sorry."

The ER doctor nodded to them to step outside. "He'll be fine. He'll need rehab, but you probably already know that."

"He'll get it," Rafa said grimly, but his face registered relief. "Is that something he can have here? If he's discharged, it'll take a miracle to get him into a facility."

"We have the ability, but we can't force him to agree. That's down to you." The doctor smiled at Noemi. "You know where to go and who to see, right, Noe?"

"I do, thank you."

She waited until they were alone, and she and Rafa sat down in the hallway while Zani was being treated. "Do you want to call your parents?"

Rafa shook his head. "This would kill them. And Zani... the one leverage I have is not telling them. I can use that to get him to agree to rehab." He looked at her. "You're very pale, Noe. Are you okay?"

She nodded but truthfully, she had begun to feel nauseous. "I think I just need some water."

He went to get some for her, putting his arm around her shoulders. "Maybe we should get you checked out too. You took a fall."

Noemi leaned against him. "Hey, if being thrown down stairs doesn't do it..."

"Don't joke about that. Look, I'm going to get someone. I'm taking a risk on you or the twins."

He got up and Noemi sat back sipped the cool water and closed her eyes. Soon enough, Rafa returned with Joan, who said, "Come on, you. Let's get you checked out."

As Joan checked her vitals, Noemi insisted that she didn't need a doctor. "I think he just caught me with his elbow and bruised my stomach. The babies feel fine."

"Well, the scan will make sure. Your vitals are good."

A few minutes later, she smiled at Noemi and Rafa. "Your babies are doing just fine. This is getting exciting, people." Noemi leaned against Rafa, relief flooding over her. Rafa kissed her forehead.

"Bepi was getting fussy." Noemi looked up to see Leo staring at the scanner, still pressed against Noemi's bare belly. Bepi was at her side. Noemi felt her heart sink.

Rafa got up and took Bepi's hand. "Thanks, Leo. Listen..."

Leo turned away. "Leo!" Noemi called out to her sister, seeing the stricken look on her face, but she couldn't get off the bed fast enough. "Rafa, go after her."

Rafa shook his head. "No, Noemi. Let her go. She needs to process this."

Noemi wasn't happy about it, but she let it go, knowing Rafa could hardly go chasing her sister through the hospital. Instead Joan helped her clean up the scanning gel, then Noemi slid from the bed, thanking her friend. She took Bepi from Rafa, wanting to hold the little boy and get some comfort. Rafa put his arms around them both. "Look, I'll stay here with Zani, try to get him to agree to rehab. Why don't I get a driver to come pick you and Bepi up to take you home? Both of you need some sleep."

21
_____

CHAPTER TWENTY-ONE

Bepi was fast asleep by the time he and Noemi arrived back at the mansion. Noemi put him to bed, stroking his little head. "I love you, little one."

Downstairs she cleared up the mess from earlier, then sat down, waiting to hear from Rafa. It was a little after midnight and she longed to try to call Leonora, wanted her to yell at her or something just so she could feel less... what did she feel? When it came down to it, Noemi hadn't gotten pregnant by design, especially not to torture Leonora. So why did she feel so guilty?

She remembered Lazlo telling her how hard it was for anyone to persuade her not to feel that guilt—maybe it was just in her genetic makeup. God, what a freakin' mess. Exhaustion set in then, and she curled up on the couch to wait for Rafa to come home.

RAFA SAT in the chair at the side of his brother's bed and waited for him to wake. To his relief, Zani was responding to treatment and had been awake and cognizant for a few minutes but had fallen back asleep.

"Better for him to sleep," the doctor had told him. "When he's asleep, he's not jonesing for a fix."

"Right."

Zani stirred now and opened his eyes. He saw Rafa sitting by him and pulled himself up against the pillows. "Rafa."

"How do you feel?"

Zani smiled ruefully. "Dumb. Stupid."

"No arguments here."

"Is Noe okay? I feel terrible."

"She's fine. The babies are fine." Rafa watched his brother's reaction. "You knew?"

Zani nodded. "I overheard. Sorry. I don't sleep so good."

"That would be the coke and God knows what else. What the fuck did you think you were doing using in my house, Zani? Where my son sleeps?"

"I am sorry, brother. I truly am. God, Rafa... do you know how hard it is to be as good as you are? I fucked up."

"You're always fucking up, Zani, and don't turn this around on me. Jesus, you've had everything, every chance, and now..." Rafa stopped, taking a deep breath, calming himself.

"Have you called Dad?"

Rafa shook his head.

"But you're going to?"

Rafa nodded. "Unless you get treatment. Here. Now. You stay here and go through rehab. Then afterwards, you can live with us but with weekly drug testing. You work for me. You straighten out your life."

Zani had a strange look on his face. "If only it was that easy, man."

"What does that mean?"

Zani just shook his head. "Look... Okay. I'll do it. Do you think I want to live like this? No. Fine. Rehab."

Rafa didn't know whether to believe him but decided to take him at face value. "Good. I mean it—you miss one session, fail one drug test, that's it. Is there anything else you want to tell me, Zani?"

"Like what?"

"Like what happened in Europe? Like the reason you came back? It wasn't just running out of money, was it?"

Zani looked away from him. "It doesn't matter now."

Driving back home, Rafa arranged for a security guard to be stationed at Zani's hospital door. "To keep him in, as well as undesirables out," he told the man.

When he got home, he found Noemi asleep in the living room. He picked her up in his arms, smiling as she stirred. "Come on, sleepy."

Noemi was awake by the time they got to their bedroom, and she pressed her lips to his. They had no need for words now. All fatigue fled as they undressed each other and climbed onto the bed.

Noemi stroked his cock until it was rock hard then Rafa pushed into her as she wrapped her legs around him. They made love slowly, their eyes locked on the other's, forging a deeper connection as they moved.

Noemi stroked his face with both hands. "I love you so much, Rafael Genova."

"You are my love," he murmured, his lips against hers, "The love of my life."

Her eyes widened, and he nodded, showing her he meant every word and tears rolled down her cheeks. He kissed them away. "We are forever now, my love. Forever."

His pace quickened as she clenched her vagina around his unrestrained, thrusting cock, and their breathing grew harsh and ragged as they both reached their climaxes. Noemi's back arched up, and Rafa took her nipple into his mouth as she moaned and writhed, sucking hard then letting out a long groan of release as his cock pumped creamy cum deep inside her. They made love once more before falling asleep just before dawn.

A few hours later, a bored Bepi crawled onto their bed and settled between them, chatty in the early morning, making them both smile. Noemi took a long shower as Rafa dressed Bepi.

It was Saturday, so they ate a leisurely brunch, and Rafa called the hospital to check in on Zani.

"Well," he told Noemi as he ended the call, "He's still there. That's progress."

Noemi smiled and smoothed his curls. "It is. I'm going to call Leo to see if she'll see me. We have to talk sooner or later."

"You should... but can I ask a favor?"

"Anything, babe."

"Could you call her later? There's something I would really like us to do, and if Bepi is with us, it might make things easier."

Noemi half-smiled. "Intriguing... what is it?"

Rafa grinned. "I think it's time, Noe. I had planned a night out for us all at a restaurant, but now I think it's important we do this today. I think it's time you met my parents."

22

CHAPTER TWENTY-TWO

Day one of rehab, and Zani was already regretting it. The specialist had been by to advise him what would happen —he was to go cold turkey—Rafa's suggestion.

"Thanks, brother." He murmured, downing a glass of cold water.

His skin felt itchy, he was dripping sweat, and irritation made him antsy and jittery. He walked to the door, then stopped when he saw the security guard Rafa had stationed outside. Zani grumbled to himself and went back to bed.

He managed a couple of hours sleep before he was awoken by the nurse checking his vitals. She smiled at him. "How are you feeling?"

"Like death."

"Good," she said brightly, "then it's working." She grinned at him, and he couldn't help chuckling.

"You're enjoying my torture."

"I admit I am, but only because I know how much better you'll feel when this is all over."

Zani's eyebrows shot up. "You?"

She smiled. "Yup. Fifteen years ago. Then I got my nursing degree, and now I torture people who went through the same thing I did. It's my penance."

Zani chuckled. "Except you enjoy it."

"I enjoy it when you get better. Now, take your poison." She handed him the painkillers, the few drugs he was still allowed. "Only to take the edge off, I'm afraid."

"Better than nothing."

"Are you hungry?"

Zani turned on the charm. "Not for food."

The nurse, Georgia, grinned. "That's all that's on offer."

"Then no thanks."

"Just keep your fluids up, and I'll be happy. Oh, and you got a card. I left it on your table."

When Georgia had gone—Zani missed her already, she was super-cute with a great rack and a butt that he could bounce coins off —he opened the envelope she had left him.

At first, he didn't understand what he was seeing: a piece of paper with a collage of photographs set out like a photo story on it. One was of a woman from a distance, taken as she was walking along a street somewhere, he guessed, in France. Her hair was dark, her body slim, dressed in a simple summer dress.

It was the next photograph that made his knees give way. The woman was laying on her back, her eyes open and staring. Sophia. Her blonde hair dyed brunette, her beautiful face lovely even in death.

Two telltale bullet holes in her torso. Blood spread across the cotton of her dress.

They had found her.

The next photographs sent chills down his spine. Rafa. Noemi. Bepi. And the words written under them...

One of them is next.

As they drove to Rafa's parents house outside of the city, Noemi squeezed her lover's thigh and smiled at him. "What are you going to tell them about Zani?"

"Nothing. Or at least I'll fudge the details. Tell them he's gone away to clear his head. I promised him that if he went through rehab, I'd protect him. Dad's a mild-mannered guy but he'd been pushed to the brink by this. As angry as I am with him, I don't want Zani's life ruined."

"You're a good man."

"Would you believe it if I told you Zani wasn't the devil either?"

Noemi smiled. "I would and I do. I believe he's genuinely sorry for what happened."

Rafa smiled. "We're here."

He turned into the driveway of his parent's estate, but it was still a few moments before the house came into view.

"Wow." Noemi gaped at the size of the place—it made Rafa's place look like a shack. "How many bedrooms does this behemoth have?"

Rafa laughed. "You really don't want to know... but it has two ballrooms."

"Because of all those pesky balls one needs to have at the exact same time," Noemi shook her head, smiling. "How the other half live."

"Says the surgeon."

Noemi snickered. "I'll let you know when I need a house the size of Bainbridge Island."

RAFA HELPED Noemi from the car and then retrieved Bepi from his car seat. Noemi took a few deep breaths. She had only ever been in the same room as Rafa's parents once, while they visited Thomasina, and although they had been introduced, she had been too occupied with Tomi to pay much attention. Hindsight is a great thing, she thought to herself now. If only I had known then that I would be giving birth to their grandchildren in a couple of years.

The thought made her giggle, and Rafa raised his eyebrows. She told him in a low voice, and he laughed as they walked to the door. "If only we had known, indeed." He took her hand. "Don't worry, sweetheart. They'll love you."

He opened the door, and rather incongruously in Noemi's opinion, called out. "Mom, Dad, it's me." Noemi hid her grin; they'd been announced by the CCTV already, she was sure.

She squeezed his hand again, and he smiled at her as his parents came to find them. Stefano Genova grinned widely. "Hey, hey, hey!"

Bepi ran up to his grandfather, and Stefano swung him into his arms. Rafael's beautiful, elegant mother, Eloise, came up to them, and kissed Rafa's cheek. "Hello my boy. And hello again, Dr. Castor... may I call you Noemi?"

"Of course, Mrs. Genova."

"Eloise. Now, Rafa tells us you have something to tell us? Why don't you all come through; we've had some food prepared and some punch."

Noemi looked at Rafa who nodded encouragingly. Yup. They were doing this. They were going to tell his parents about the twins. She held Rafa's hand tighter.

She couldn't help the gasp when Eloise and Stefano led them out onto the patio. The grounds were huge and beautifully landscaped. Noemi realized she was gaping when Eloise chuckled. "I'll take that as a compliment, dear."

"You should! Your home, these grounds, wow." Noemi knew she sounded starstruck, but the place was sensational. Suddenly she felt like an outsider, and a jolt shot through her. What was she doing in this world?

Luckily no one else seemed to pick up on her discomfort, and soon they were sitting down, Bepi happily playing with his grandparent's dogs, and Rafa was taking Noemi's hand. "Mom, Dad, I won't keep you in the dark any longer... you're going to be grandparents again. We both know it's crazy fast, but Noemi has made me and Bepi so very happy. I hope you will give us your blessing."

Stefano and Eloise looked at each other and for a moment, Noemi had a nightmare vision of them throwing her from the house for 'trapping' their son. Instead the older couple beamed and embraced them both. "Darlings, we're so happy for you."

Noemi was relieved, but she still felt as though something was being unsaid. She waited until Rafa and Stefano were strolling around the grounds to speak to Eloise.

"Eloise... I know this must be a surprise to you, especially with me being Thomasina's surgeon. I assure you, my relationship with Rafa began way, way after Tomi passed."

Eloise smiled. "What makes me think you've been practicing that line?"

"It's not a line—"

Eloise held her hands up. "I meant no malice by that. What I meant was you seem desperate to convince us that you didn't start a relationship with Rafa by design. Darling... we already know that. Rafa has spoken to us about your romance, and believe me, my son is an excellent judge of character. If he had thought that you weren't genuine in any way, he wouldn't be with you." She patted Noemi's hand. "Don't be so hard on yourself. You're a successful surgeon, a career woman. Rafa is very lucky."

Noemi felt her anxiety lessen, and she smiled at the other woman. "I love him so much. You raised an incredible man."

Eloise thanked her then sighed. "If only I could have raised two such men."

"Zani?"

Eloise nodded. "He's not a bad man, nor a vicious one; he's just... rootless. Our money spoiled him."

"Maybe in time, he'll calm down?" Noemi wished she could reassure the other woman, but Rafa had made a promise to his brother, and she wasn't about to break that promise for him.

"He's forty-three, Noemi, I think his time to calm down was about twenty years ago. Do you have siblings, Noemi?"

Noemi nodded, swallowing the lump in her throat. She needed to call Leo, to try to explain what was going on. "I do. A sister. Adoptive sister—I was adopted by my family—but we're very close." She hoped that wasn't a lie now.

They spent a couple of hours with Rafa's parents before traveling home. Rafa had supper with them before excusing himself to go to the hospital. "I won't be long, honey. If you want to go see your sister when I get back, I can drive you?"

Noemi shook her head. "I'll call her. I expect she won't want to see me yet."

Rafa kissed her forehead. "In that case, I might go to the office to make sure everything is good there. Do you mind?"

"Not at all, baby. Bepi and I will play some games, maybe do some reading."

"Momma Bear."

She grinned. "It's good practice. Besides, I've been neglecting Mouse too. We'll have some fun out in the yard."

Rafa kissed her. "Take care of our babies in there."

"I will."

NOEMI PLAYED with Bepi and Mouse until both the dog and the boy were exhausted, then as they cuddled up with her on the couch, she called Leo.

At first, she didn't think her sister would pick up, then as she was about to end the call, she heard her voice. "This isn't a good time."

Noemi drew in a deep breath. "Then tell me when a good time would be, Leo. We need to talk."

"No, I don't think we do, Noe. There's nothing to talk about. You're pregnant and I'm alone. Once again, you win."

That hurt. "Once again? What are you talking about? No one wins; this isn't a game. I didn't get pregnant to torment you, or to win a competition only you seem to be in."

"Then how come you get the handsome billionaire, the ready-made family, the beautiful baby? I got squat. My child was taken from me, and there's no one to comfort me."

"You have us, your family, your—"

The line went dead, and Noemi sighed. Leo was hurting, she knew. Her sister wasn't a spiteful person and didn't normally feel sorry for herself, but maybe this time she was entitled to feel aggrieved.

"Not that we did anything wrong," Noemi whispered, her hand splayed out over her belly. "But maybe Leo's entitled to be angry for a while. That's okay, we can take it, can't we?"

She looked down at Bepi's little head, resting against her thigh, his thumb stuck in his mouth as he slept. He might not be my son, she thought as she stroked his curls, but I would die for this little tyke. She glanced at the clock. Almost eight p.m. The house was silent, peaceful. Noemi knew she should really put Bepi to bed, but it was so comfortable here on the couch, and Bepi and her dog were sleeping so soundly...

Noemi closed her eyes and let sleep come. She woke, confused a couple of hours later when Rafa's head of security came to find her, pale-faced and shaken, to tell her there had been an explosion at Rafa's office.

CHAPTER TWENTY-THREE

Hysteria was near as she ran through the hospital, Bepi in her arms. It was only when she saw Kit, obviously sent to find her, that she relaxed. Kit was holding his hands up, calming her, a smile on his face. "He's okay; he's fine. We're just checking him out."

Noemi didn't know what to say as she followed Kit to the ER. When she saw Rafa, she gave a cry of distress, and shielded Bepi. Rafa shook his head, smiling ruefully. Blood streaked down his face from a cut on his forehead. "Looks worse than it is, babe. They're just going to clean it up."

Noemi nodded and took Bepi from the room until they told her Rafa was ready. She walked back in, and Rafa kissed her.

"I'm really okay," he said in a low voice, leaning the unhurt part of his forehead against hers. "Thankfully, I was the only one left in the office."

"What happened?"

Rafa shook his head. "I couldn't tell you. One minute I'm walking to the copy machine, the next I'm flying through the air. They think it was a device in my office."

Noemi's body went ice cold. "A bomb?"

"We don't know, but it looks like something like that, yeah."

"Oh, God, Rafa... Rafa..." She sank down on the gurney next to him. Rafa took Bepi from her arms.

"Noe, breathe."

"Why are you so calm? Someone tried to k—" Noemi clamped her mouth shut, mindful of Bepi's presence, but she couldn't help the tears rolling down her face. "Why?"

Rafa cut his eyes to his son, and she nodded. Later. She found she couldn't stop trembling. His face—his beautiful face—was covered in cuts and bruises, his left hand bandaged now.

They heard voices from the hallway, and his parents came into the room, both pale and scared. Rafa reassured them that he was fine. "Look, let's get out of here and we'll talk about it at home."

BACK AT THE MANSION, they put Bepi to bed and settled in the living room. Rafa looked exhausted, but Noemi knew he wanted to reassure them. "Look, any business has enemies."

Stefano made a noise. "Enemies, yes, but this is a little more than that, son."

"Look, if whoever it was really wanted me dead, I'd be dead. I think this was just a warning."

"Yes, but from whom?" His mother looked on the edge of tears.

"I don't know, Mom. Look, the police, the FBI, they're all looking into it. I suspect over the next few days I'll be talking a lot to them. The office is uninhabitable, so I'll work from home and you know there's plenty of security here."

"Keep Bepi home from school for a few days."

"I will."

AFTER HIS PARENTS had finally been persuaded that he was safe and well, Rafa and Noemi shared a soak in his tub. Noemi washed his cuts, kissing each one as he smiled at her. His hands cupped her breasts, thumbs stroking over her nipples. Even this early on in her pregnancy, her breasts were fuller, riper, and with her dark hair hanging in damp strands down her back, she looked almost ethereal.

"You're so beautiful," he said, and she smiled shyly.

"As long as you think so."

She smoothed his curls back from his face, her brown eyes full of love and concern. "If anything had happened to you..."

"I'm fine; I'm good." He felt like a parrot, repeating the same thing.

"Rafa?"

"Yes, babe?"

Noemi sighed, hesitating. "There's something I didn't tell you. I didn't think it was worth... no, that's not true, I just..."

Rafa grinned. "Just tell me, boo."

She took a deep breath in. "A few weeks ago, the day I told you we were having twins, I had an argument with a guy at Alki Beach. He was being a creeper, and I told him where to get off. No biggie, it happens to us women all the time. Later, though, after I came to your office, I went back to the car, and there was a Polaroid picture left on my windshield."

"Of?"

"Of me. In the baby store earlier that day."

Rafa felt the shock of her revelation. "What? Why didn't you tell me?"

"Because, truthfully, nothing came of it."

"But someone was watching you?"

"Must have been. Nothing has happened since but with the bombing... maybe we should be more vigilant."

Rafa sat in silence for a long time, thinking. He would give all the money in the world that this was something to do with Zani's dealings in Europe. Had Zani gotten involved with some psycho drug dealers? He wouldn't put it past his brother. The thought of Noemi being stalked made him feel sick. "Tomorrow, first thing, I'm going to get the FBI involved. Do you still have the photograph?"

She nodded. "Yes, and I have a picture of the guy who harassed me in the park."

Rafa smiled. "Good girl. God, Noe, why didn't you tell me?"

"We had other things to talk about." She pressed her lips to his. "You must be exhausted."

Rafa smiled, his lips curving up against hers. "I could be more tired..."

Noemi chuckled. "Are you sure? I mean, you've been through a traumatic experience and..." She grinned mischievously, "...you're not a young man anymore and... oww, oww, stop!"

She giggled as he tickled her in retribution for her teasing then he lifted her onto his lap, his cock responding to her touch as she reached between his legs. "Baby, if nothing else, you know how to make me feel better."

Noemi chuckled. "Nothing like a good screw after a bombing." She winced. "No, nope. Not ready to make jokes about it yet."

"Hey, hey, I'm here. Nothing's going to take me away from you and our children. Nothing." He cupped her cheek, but Noemi shook her head.

"No jokes. This is serious, baby."

Rafa sighed, lifting her off of his lap, his erection fading. "I admit, I'm weary. What a day."

"I can make you relax, baby. Let's go to bed, and you can sleep."

They went to bed and held each other, talking quietly until they fell asleep.

Noemi opened her eyes. The moon shone through the open drapes, casting a blue light in the room. Rafa was asleep, his face turned towards her, his arm around her waist. Noemi watched him sleep for a while, stroking his cheek gently then slipped from the bed.

She checked in on Bepi, seeing he was fast asleep, then walked to the farthest corner of the house. Only then did she let herself break down. The attempt on Rafa's life had been the last straw, and now she buried her face in her hands and sobbed quietly, releasing all the pent-up emotion from the last few months.

Mouse padded quietly to her owner, nudging her hand with her muzzle, and Noemi hugged the dog to her, burying her face in her fur as she cried. Mouse seemed to sense Noemi needed comfort in the way all dogs seem to know by instinct and licked her face. Noemi half-laughed, half-cried. "Oh, Mousie... I can't lose him."

Noemi cried herself out and then got up and walked to the kitchen, splashing water on her face. She let Mouse out to pee and stood in the doorway, breathing in the cool night air. Rafa is okay. He's not hurt... much. She guessed he would ache in the morning from being hurled across the room by the blast but that was a small price to pay for survival. Who the hell would want to kill Rafa?

Noemi tried to figure out why anyone would want to hurt Rafael Genova, the sweetest man she had ever met. A suspicion had started in her mind about Zani's mysterious time in Europe, but she hadn't wanted to ask Rafa what he thought. They had enough trouble with Zani as it was.

There was the creep in the park, but she was sure he was just a douche bag who thought he could intimidate a lone woman. The photos disturbed her, but Seattle wasn't that big a city... maybe he had followed her, taken the photos...

"Don't be absurd." She rubbed her face and sighed.

"Can't you sleep?"

Rafa's voice was low as he padded quietly to her. She shook her head, gazing up at him, stroking his cheek.

He smiled down at her then bent his head to press his lips against hers. Noemi slid her hands over his bare chest, and when he broke away, his eyes were questioning.

She nodded, and he picked her up, setting her down on the counter and pushing her robe apart. He sucked on her nipple while his hand slid between her legs, his thumb fingering her clit as he slid two fingers deep inside her. Noemi ground against his hand, curving her legs around his waist, her own hands stroking his cock into a state of such hardness it was no effort to thrust into her.

Rafa gently pushed her down and tugged her hips closer, slamming into her as she writhed with pleasure. He stroked her belly, caressing her breasts as he fucked her, and Noemi repaid his love by tightening her thighs and her cunt, contracting around his cock as it plowed deep into her.

He drove her to a shattering climax, and Noemi had to muffle her cry of ecstasy. Rafa, coming hard, triumphantly, slid her to her feet and turned her around, bending her over the counter.

Noemi gasped as he eased into her ass, panting hard as he made love to her, curving her body up against his, her legs spread wide. Rafa's lips were on her neck, biting, sucking, kissing, tasting her skin. He made her come again, then they lay together on the cold tile floor, as the breeze from the window blew in.

Noemi turned her head to gaze at him, but they had no need for words now. Rafa stroked her face lightly with the tip of his finger, and she nodded—a silent assent. They would make it through this.

Whatever it took.

CHAPTER TWENTY-FOUR

*Z*ani Genova shifted impatiently in his chair. Group sessions were the worst. He hated sitting here in this room with these other addicts telling stories of their habits. He couldn't tell the truth about his.

He looked around the room as another attendee was speaking. They were good people who got lost. He, on the other hand, knew he was the scum of the earth, someone whose cowardice knew no bounds.

When they'd told him an attempt on Rafa's life had been made, that had been the moment to come clean. Tell his security team, tell the police, the FBI. Tell Rafa. It was because of him, Zani, that he had nearly lost his life.

And yet he had stayed silent, still looking after number one—again. It had already cost Sophie her life... Zani was disgusted with himself. What if Bepi had been at the office? He was sure the little boy would not have survived a blast. What if someone delivered a package to the house? Bepi, Rafa, Noemi...

He was still remonstrating with himself when he got back to his room, still arguing about it in his head when the door opened, and Noemi greeted him with a sweet smile. She really was a cutie.

"Hey, Zani, how're you feeling? Docs tell me you're doing well?"

No. No, I'm not, and you could die because of me, lovely lady... "I'm good. Getting clean was the only way left, really. How's Rafa?"

Her smile faded a little. "He's okay. A little muscle soreness from being thrown around but apart from that, he's good." She sighed. Zani thought her eyes looked a little puffy, and there was a deep line between her eyes.

"Hey," he said, forcing a smile. "Never seen you in your doctor gear before."

She was wearing her white coat with Dr. Noemi Castor embroidered on the pocket. Noemi nodded. "Time to get back to work. Stops me obsessing about who the hell would want to hurt Rafa." She looked down at her hands, then shot a glance at Zani. "You don't have any ideas, do you?"

Zani felt dismay flood through him. Tell her. Tell her and maybe you'll save everyone's lives. "Noemi..." Images of Sophie's dead body floated through his mind. "No," he said, looking away from her. "I don't."

He couldn't bear to look at his brother's lover. "Noe, I'm pretty bushed."

Noemi got up, her lovely face sad. "Of course. I'll come by later... if you want to talk."

NOEMI PERFORMED two simple surgeries on her first day back and was glad she got through them without complications. Her head wasn't entirely in the game yet. She updated her charts then went downstairs to take some blood samples to the lab.

The lab was in the oldest part of the hospital, and the doctors and nurses had long nicknamed it 'The Crypt'. The long hallway that led down to the lab had lighting which was temperamental to say the least, and Noemi cussed softly now as the florescent tubes flickered and went out. It was pitch black, but luckily it was a straight walk to the lab. She ran her hand along the wall until she reached the lab door and pushed against it.

Locked. She frowned. Odd. She banged on the door. "Geoff?" She called out to the lab technician she knew was on duty this evening. "Geoff, it's Noe. Can you let me in?"

No answer. At the far end of the hall, the door opened and closed before she could see who had entered through it. "Hey, can you see if the light switch will work? No one's in the lab."

No answer. Her heart began to beat a little faster. "Hey?"

She could hear footsteps but no one answered her. Noemi backed up against the lab door. "Geoff? If you're in there, now would be a great time to open the door." She kept her tone light, but her voice shook.

He or she was close now; she could hear them breathing. "Come on, man, talk to me. This isn't funny."

She wasn't ready for the punch to her stomach, and it knocked the breath out of her lungs. She doubled up, her arms folding protective over her abdomen. "Please," she gasped, "I'm pregnant."

Her attacker grabbed her hair and threw her to the ground. Noemi curled up in a ball. To her great relief, her attacker took off, and she heard the door at the end of the hallway slam open as he or she made their escape. Noemi staggered to her feet and made her way back to the main hospital. Her stomach was screeching with pain, but she only cared about her babies. She ignored the startled look of her colleagues as she ran passed them, towards the gynecological department.

"Someone just attacked me, punched me in the belly, and I'm pregnant," she said in a rush to the first nurse she saw. "I need someone to do a scan, to check me out. Please."

The nurse, her expression shocked, steered Noemi into a chair. "Okay, Doctor. Just breathe for me, and I'll go find Dr. Hallsback. Just, please sit for me and take some deep breaths. We'll look after you."

Noemi did as she was told, wrapped her arms around her stomach. Please be okay. It had all happened so quickly that she was still processing it. What the hell? She felt a wave of lightheadedness sweep over her, and she swayed. God, don't faint, don't faint...

She felt a dampness seeping down her legs. Oh, no, please don't be blood... that could only mean one thing.

"Noe?" James Hallsback, one of the Gynecology Attendings came to see her, but as she tried to speak, dark spots gathered in her vision, and she passed out into his arms.

JAMES HALLSBACK YELLED for help and picked up Noemi's slight body, carrying her into one of the rooms. "What the hell happened?"

"She said she was attacked, that she was punched. Doctor..." The nurse indicated the sheet—blood. "She's pregnant."

"Right." He went into emergency mode, ordering blood, saline, and tests. "And bring me a scanner, stat."

He leaned over Noemi. "Noe? Noe? Can you hear me? Open your eyes, sweetheart, we've got you."

Noemi stirred. "Pain," she whispered.

"I know, sweetheart, but we're going to help you. How far along are you?"

"Eight weeks."

"Alright, darling, hold on." The nurse pushed the scanner into the room.

"I'm bleeding," Noemi said, her voice barely a whisper, "I can smell the blood."

Hallsback pushed up her black T-shirt and stopped. In a voice that shook, he turned to the nurse. "Get an OR ready right now."

"What is it? Is it my babies?"

Hallsback leaned over her again, his expression one of shock and disbelief. "No, sweetheart. You're not miscarrying... at least, that's not why you're bleeding."

Noemi looked confused. "Then why?"

Hallsback steeled himself. He couldn't believe he was about to say. "Noemi, I'm sorry but you've been stabbed, and you're bleeding badly. We have to get you into surgery right now."

. . .

Rafael Genova walked calmly although his rage was white hot and murderous. He kicked open his brother's hospital door, seeing Zani jump out of his skin. Rafa was grimly satisfied. Zani gaped at him. "What is it?"

"You are going to tell me right now what the fuck went on in Europe, and why the mother of my twins is currently being operated on for a stab wound to her belly. You're going to tell me everything, Zani, or God help me, I'll kill you myself."

He grabbed his brother's shirt and got in his face. "And if Noemi or my children die... God help you, Zani. God help you."

CHAPTER TWENTY-FIVE

Noemi opened her eyes and realized that she felt... okay. Even good. How the hell was that possible? She wasn't even sore, but she put that down to the morphine they must have given her. Rafa was sitting by her bed. "Hey, buddy."

His smile was relieved. "Hey, kiddo." He kissed her. "Thanks for the scare."

"Sorry. The twins?"

"They're fine, growing and healthy. The stab wound wasn't even that deep, thank God. Maybe a centimeter or two deep. Docs and the police think it was a warning rather than a murder attempt—not that it makes it any more acceptable."

Noemi pulled herself into a sitting position and drew in a deep breath. "But putting together this and the bombing..."

Rafa nodded, his face grim. "Zani."

"He's admitted something?"

"Singing like a bird to the FBI. Interpol is getting involved. Seems my delightful brother owes money to some psycho drug lords in Italy. They killed his ex-girlfriend."

Noemi felt cold. "God."

Rafa took her hand. "Noe... the FBI thinks we may have to go into protective custody. The people Zani is mixed up with... their reach is wide and deadly."

"What do they want?"

"Zani." Rafa sighed. "And it's an impossible situation. If he goes to them, he's a dead man. If not, then we have to go into protective custody in order to survive. You and I and Bepi. My parents. Your parents. Leo. Possible even more."

Noemi looked at him, appalled. Solomon's choice. "Oh, God, Rafa."

"I know."

Noemi put a hand over her belly protectively. "What did he do to them?"

"He took their drugs, enough to stop an army, and never paid for them. You don't fuck around with organized crime in Italy. And Zani knew that. Knows that." He pinched the bridge of his nose, wincing at the thought of using past tense about his only brother.

Noemi took his hand in hers. "Do they want money?"

Rafa shook his head. "We simply don't know. The FBI have told me to trust them, but they don't know these people. I've used contacts, reached out. If they want money, they can have it—every penny if they leave us in peace, but I don't know if they'll be satisfied with it."

There was a knock at the door and Zani's security guard came in, his face grim. "I'm sorry to interrupt, but you have to come now, Mr. Genova."

Rafa stood, alarmed. "What is it?"

"It's Zani, sir. He's on the roof."

RAFA WAS LED out onto the roof and immediately saw his brother standing on the very edge of it. "Zani..."

Zani turned, his expression one of desolation and shame. "I'm so sorry, Rafa. I never wanted any of this. I was arrogant and complacent, and it cost Sophia her life. They'll keep coming for you, Rafa, and Noe and Bepi, and I can't...I have to take myself out of the equation. They'll stop if I'm dead."

Rafa shook his head. "No, they won't, Zani. Not this way. They'll feel cheated, and the price they'll force us to pay will be too high. This is not the way."

Zani swayed and the various people who had gathered to save him caught their breath. "They hurt your girl, Rafa. They tried to kill you. They will never stop."

"They will. They will." Rafa was struggling to keep his voice calm, but he was terrified. Zani looked beyond hope. "Everyone has a price, Zani. I'll give them every penny I have to leave us alone. But it won't come to that. The FBI, Interpol... the authorities in Italy. They want to take them down too. We're working together. Your death will only hinder that. We need your testimony, Zani. Just think, with your help, we can bring them down, make them pay for Sophia's murder."

Zani squeezed his eyes shut. "When you told me they'd stabbed Noemi..."

"Noemi is fine. The twins are fine. They won't be if you jump."

"He's right, Zani."

Rafa turned to see Noemi, being pushed in a wheelchair by Lazlo Merchant out onto the roof —clearly the only way Lazlo would let her leave her hospital bed. She took Rafa's hand, but kept her gaze on Zani, whose face softened when he saw her.

"Noe... I'm so sorry."

"It's not your fault. And Rafa's right, I'm fine; it was barely a scratch. Just looked worse than it was. But you will hurt me, hurt Rafa, hurt your wonderful parents if you jump. Please, Zani. No one wants this. No one. It will be such a waste, and for no reason. Don't let those scumbags win."

"I'm the scumbag, Noemi."

"No. You fucked up, yes, but God, Zani, who hasn't? I know I have, over and over and over, and you know what? I'll fuck up again. That's life. We can get through this—together. We are a family now. And now I'm going to use the best excuse for you to stay alive, and yes, it's totally manipulative. Don't let Bepi or the twins grow up without their uncle. They need you."

A faint smile crossed his face. "You're right, that is manipulative."

Noemi fixed him with a stare. "I don't care. Please, Zani... for them. Come away from the edge, and we'll face whatever we have to together."

It seemed like an age had passed, but finally, Zani stepped away from the edge. Rafa felt weak with relief and eternally grateful to the woman he loved. Noemi held her free hand out to Zani and he took it. Noemi struggled to her feet and hugged Zani. Zani buried his face in her hair, and Rafa heard him sob, saw his shoulders shaking. Noemi held his brother tightly, whispering comforting words into his ear until Zani was able to calm himself.

DOWNSTAIRS, they sat in Zani's room. "Call Mom and Dad, please, Rafa," he said, looking exhausted. "It's time I faced up to what I've done."

"Fine. The FBI want to talk to you again, and I think we ought to crank up all of our security." Rafa stroked Noemi's hair. "Do you mind if I step out for a few minutes?"

"Not at all, babe."

Left alone with Zani, Noemi suddenly felt shy. "Zani, we don't know each other that well, but can we start again? I'd like to help you."

"I don't deserve that, Noe, but thank you. I'll take all the help I can get." He nodded at her. "How are you feeling? Really?"

"Honestly, it's nothing. The worse thing was not knowing what was happening."

"How did it happen?"

Noemi told him about the locked lab door and the dark hallway. "Huh." Zane looked confused.

"What?"

"No, it's just... if it was my enemies, they wouldn't have hidden in the shadows. They would want you to know who it was who was attacking you. And I hate to say it, but I doubt you would have gotten away so lightly."

Noemi paled. "God."

"I'm sorry, Noe. It could have been a drug addict."

Noemi remembered the break-in at her apartment. Whore. Could it be that her enemy was separate from the Genova's? Jesus. Somehow, she hoped not because she had no idea who would want to harm her otherwise.

She rubbed her face, sighing. "I'm at a loss, Zani. These past few months... Hell, these past two years have been crazy. Both ends of the spectrum, crazy good and crazy bad."

Zani smiled at her. "I know the feeling."

NOEMI REFUSED to stay overnight in hospital. "No, it's just a small wound and I'm fine."

Lazlo and Dr Hallsback weren't happy, but they couldn't insist she stay.

Rafa took her home. Rafa's parents had taken Bepi for the night, and Rafa made Noemi take a long bath while he made her some food.

She padded out into the kitchen, wrapped in a robe and he put his arms around her. "Feel better?"

"Much." She kissed him. "You could have joined me."

Rafa grinned. "If I had, we'd still be in that bath, and my cock would be buried inside your sweet cunt. And that wouldn't be the best thing for those stitches."

Noemi pulled a face. "Two stitches, Two. Everyone made a big deal about an inch-deep wound. And I want your cock buried inside me. That sounded weird, but you started it."

He laughed and drew her close. "God, I love you."

His lips found hers, then he sighed and leaned his forehead against hers. "You know what's weird?"

"What?"

"Now that we know who's targeting us, I just feel relief. We can do something about it; we know what they want. We have control back."

Noemi felt her heart sink. She stepped away from him, her hands trembling. Rafa noticed. "What is it?"

She told him about Zani's theory. "The more I think about it, the more it makes sense. Someone else is trying to mess with me."

Rafa frowned. "So, someone broke into your house and left you a message, a guy at the park stalked you, someone left a photo of you on your car. And now someone stabbed you."

"Barely, but yes."

Rafa was silent for a long time. "So, who?"

Noemi shook her head. "That's just it... I don't know."

"Let's look at this logically." Rafa took her hand, and they sat down on the couch. "Any lost patients with relatives that blame you?"

Noemi looked at him, and he realized what he'd said. "Well, you can rule out me..." He stopped. "Drew."

"No. No way. He's a man of God, for Chrissakes, and I swear, he's been nothing but kind." Noemi felt her face flame. "He spoke very highly of you... eventually."

"Misdirection? I'm not saying it is him but the timing's right." Rafa looked at her. "Are you crying?"

"Hormones." But she was lying, and Rafa knew it. "Look, I just don't want it to be him, okay? I thought I was a good judge of character."

"Alright, leave him aside—but I'm not ruling him out. Who else? The guy in the park?"

Noemi grabbed her phone and flick through to the photo. They'd already shown it to the police. "Look at him again. Do you recognize him?"

"No. You said he had an American accent?"

"Yup. He was a delight, but he had no real reason to attack me."

Rafa ran his hand through his hair, frustrated. "What I don't understand is how the attacker managed to duck every camera in the hospital. And how the hell they knew that the lab door would be locked. None of this makes sense."

"Tell me about it." Noemi curled her body into his. "I don't want to think about it anymore tonight."

Rafa out his arms around her. "You're safe here."

Noemi looked up at him. "I love you, Rafael Genova."

He smiled and kissed her gently. "And I love you. When all this is over, we can start planning our future and I swear, Noc, it will be the happiest future that I'm able to give you."

Noemi wrapped her arms around his neck. "Rafa?"

"Yes, babe?"

"Take me to bed."

Rafa grinned. "Stitches," he reminded her, and she grumbled.

"Screw the stitches... I want you. I'll go on top."

Rafa gave a dramatic sigh. "Such a wanton woman."

"You made me this way," she chuckled. Her smile faded as she gazed at him. "Tell me everything will be okay."

"I promise, my darling. It will be."

CHAPTER TWENTY-SIX

E ven with his promise, Rafa didn't expect any progress on Zani's case soon, but he was surprised when the FBI turned up the next morning. Agent Dean shook his hand. "We have news."

Agent Dean and his partner asked Rafa and Noemi to join them at the hospital. Zani was waiting for them. "You know what this is about?" He asked Rafa in a low voice. His brother shook his head.

"Nope, they just asked us to come here."

"Mr. Genova, both of you, sirs, and Ms.... sorry, Dr. Castor, I think we have good news for you. Mr. Genova... Zani, the syndicate you were involved with—"

"—nice way to put it. Mob would be more suitable," Zani said with a wry smile.

"Fair enough," Agent Dean said. "Interpol has had them under surveillance for a long time. They were running an undercover operation long before you got involved with the Syn—mob. An informant, someone close to the head of the family, had been working with them to bring the family down. That informant was tasked by the top to find you and intimidate you. He admitted planting the bomb in your office, sir," he looked at Rafa, "but also admitted to not using as much explosive as he was told too. He says he did the bare minimum, so it would please his bosses without committing murder. He denies anything to do with the attack on Dr. Castor, although he admits leaving a photograph on your car to intimidate you and sending a text message."

Rafa and Noemi looked at each other. Oh God damn it, Noemi thought. We were right. It's someone else.

Agent Dean didn't see their reaction and continued. "Long story short... unless he wants his cover blown, he's going to have to bring a result for the head of the family. Which means money or blood."

Zani stared at him. "So... we can pay off the debt, and that would be that?"

"Yes, and it's what Interpol wants. They don't want their entire operation blown by drug money."

Zani looked at Rafa. Rafa nodded. "Then it's a no brainer. I'll arrange for the money to be wired to whatever account they want. I just want my family safe."

"We'll get it done. We'll be in touch."

WHEN THE GENOVAS and Noemi were alone, Rafa looked at his brother. "It's over."

Zani shook his head. "I don't believe it. I don't."

"Did you think it would end in gun fights? Not the way the world works. Everybody has their price."

Zani rubbed his face. "I can't thank you enough."

"Yes, you can. You're getting clean. Stay that way forever. One slip and I'm out, Zani. You put my family, my son, and Noemi in danger. Let this be an end to it."

"I swear on my life, brother."

Rafa nodded stiffly. "I'll look forward to seeing it."

Zani looked at Noemi. "I promise you, too, Noe. Did you tell Rafa?"

She nodded. "We're trying to figure out who would have a grudge."

"Have you called Drew?"

Noemi looked at Rafa. "Not yet but I will." She looked at Zani. "Rafa thinks maybe Drew Ballentine."

"That would make sense."

"Have you met him?"

Zani shook his head. "No, actually. But he's the most likely suspect."

"He's a minister."

Zani gave a crooked grin. "Well, we've all heard stories about them."

As they left the hospital, Noemi turned to Rafa. "Listen, I'm going to go over to Leo's house to bang on her door until she lets me in. If today has shown me anything, it's that her love is worth fighting for."

Rafa kissed her. "Want me to come with?"

She shook her head. "We need sister time."

Noemi took a cab to Leo's house. She knocked on the door and tried to open it, but there was no answer. Leo's car was in the driveway. Noemi sighed heavily. Leo was in and ignoring her. Well, tough, lady. I'm coming in whether you want me to or not.

Noemi walked around to the garden gate and let herself in. As she walked around the side of the house, she noticed the small sapling that had been donated in Jack's name was gone, ripped out of the ground and thrown aside. Her heart sunk. Maybe Leo had lost it completely in her grief.

Suddenly the need to get into the house was imperative. Noemi banged on the back door. "Leo! It's me. I'm coming in."

The door was locked, but she found a brick and smashed the window, reaching in gingerly to unlock the door. "Leo, sorry about the glass but if you won't answer the door..."

She walked in. The air in the house was musty and stale, and Noemi's heart began to beat a little faster. "Leo?"

She moved through the utility room into the kitchen and stopped. The counter tops were full of bowls of cereal, uneaten. God. Noemi didn't need to count them to know there was one for every breakfast time since Jack died. Oh Jesus... Noemi's heart ached for her sister.

"Leo..."

She walked into the living room which was in disarray but couldn't find her sister. She went up to the second floor, checking the bedrooms. In Jack's room, she gave a cry of distress as she saw her sister lying face down on the bed. "Leo!"

She darted to her sister and turned her over. To her relief Leonora was breathing, but to her horror, her face was a bloody mess of cuts and welts.

"Leo, my God, what happened?"

Leonora opened her eyes and terror crept into them. "No, no, Noemi, please, run... he's crazy, he's crazy..."

Noemi's adrenaline spiked. "Who? Who's crazy? Who did this to you?"

Leo's eyes were whirling in her head, such was her distress. "Paul... Paul's crazy... Noemi, please... he's in the house. He's in the house."

Noemi's adrenaline was pumping hard. "Then we have to get you out of here."

She slid her arm under Leo and managed to get her to sit up. As she moved to pick her up, Leo's eyes widened, and she whimpered in fear, staring over Noemi's shoulder.

Before she could turn around, she felt the muzzle of a gun being pressed into the small of her back.

"Don't move, Noemi," Paul said in a soft voice, "or I'll blow those kids right out of your belly."

Noemi went ice cold as she heard the safety being flicked off and realized, finally, who had tried to kill her.

CHAPTER TWENTY-SEVEN

Rafa nodded at Drew Ballentine as he walked into the diner and sat down opposite him. "Drew."

"Rafa, it's good to see you."

"Is it?"

Drew put down the coffee he was about to sip. "Ah. This isn't a friendly visit. What's on your mind, Rafa?"

Rafa studied him for a moment before answering.

"Are you stalking Noemi for some reason? Did you attack and stab her, knowing she was carrying my children?"

Drew's eyes grew big. "Wow, Rafa. That, I wasn't expecting."

"Answer my question, please." Rafa's anger was on a knife-edge. Drew put his coffee cup down and placed his hands flat on the table.

"No, Rafa, of course not. Of course I would never hurt Noemi, or anyone else. Why on earth would you think that?"

Rafa told him everything in a flat, dead tone. "So, you can see why I might be suspicious."

Drew nodded slowly. "Now that you put it like that... yes, I suppose you would think of me, especially when I made a deliberate effort to insert myself into Noemi's life. But no, I swear to you. I would never stoop so low. Was I surprised when Noemi told me about the two of you? Yes, I admit I was. Was there a fleeting moment of thinking that your relationship was inappropriate? Yes, for a scintilla. But your relationship is entirely your business and knowing Noemi now, I think Thomasina would be delighted for the both of you."

He let out a shaky breath and for the first time, Rafa saw real emotion in him. "I'm sorry to hear about Noemi. Is she alright?"

"Yes, thankfully. The stabbing wasn't serious, and both she and the babies are doing well. But you can see why I'm trying to figure out who would do this to her."

"I can, but I will swear on the Bible, it wasn't me. I'll take a polygraph, give DNA, anything. When did it happen?"

Rafa told him and Drew visibly relaxed. "That day, I can tell you I had a workshop, all day at one of the smaller chapels in the city. Bereavement counseling. There was a small group, but I took individual sessions both in the morning and in the evening. You can check with the participants; I'm sure they wouldn't mind speaking on my behalf."

Rafa couldn't decide whether he was being played, but his gut told him Ballentine was on the level. "Maybe a couple."

"No problem, although there was one man I'd rather you didn't call. He was a very disturbed young man: angry, combative. He told me that he'd just lost his six-year-old son, and he blamed the mother and her family for not letting him be in the kid's life."

Rafa's skin prickled. "What?"

Drew didn't pick up on Rafa's concern. "I can't name names obviously, but I saw the kind of anger you're talking about. Mental health in this country..."

Rafa held up his hand, stopping him, his eyes almost wild with terror. "Drew, was this guy's name Paul?"

Drew's expression told him everything he needed to know, and Rafa cursed loudly, drawing the attention of the other patrons. Rafa stood, but Drew was too quick for him. "What is it? What is it, Rafa?"

"It's Noemi's sister's ex. The father of her nephew who died. Jack... Drew, he was six years old and barely knew his father..."

Realization dawned and Drew look horrified. "Oh, dear God Rafa..."

"I have to find Noemi."

Drew nodded. "Let me drive. You're in no condition... Come on, Rafa. Let's go find your girl."

"Turn around, Noemi."

Noemi did as she was told, keeping hold of Leonora's hand. Paul smiled at her, but his eyes were cold, dead. He kept the gun leveled at the center of her belly, and Noemi couldn't help but put her hand over it protectively, knowing that if he shot her, she could do nothing to protect her babies. "Paul..."

"Shut up. I do the talking. Six years of talking I'm owed." He looked at Leonora. "None of you let me see him until the day I got to kiss his cold little face. In his coffin! God..."

"We never stopped you visiting—"

Paul cold-cocked Noemi, and she fell back as Leonora screamed. Noemi's head spun and screeched with pain as she gasped, but she was determined not to lose consciousness. Paul aimed the gun at her head. "Shut your lying mouth, Noemi, just shut up. I should have finished what I started in that hallway."

Noemi swallowed. "Why didn't you? Why didn't you kill me then?"

"Because..." He spat at her, but she saw the flicker of his eyes towards her stomach. Because I told him I was pregnant...

It gave her hope. "Did you break into my apartment?"

Paul smiled. "I did. I was only looking for information on Jack's whereabouts. I had to improvise when I heard someone coming. Plus, I saw you with Rafael Genova. Gold-digging whore..."

Noemi was confused, ignoring his jibe. "Paul, no one stopped you seeing Jack apart from yourself."

He laughed. "You can really sit there and say that? Noemi, please. You, Leo, your parents... all of you conspired to keep my son from me."

"Bullshit." Noemi was angry now. "You are the definition of deadbeat dad, Paul. Jack would have loved you to be—" She had shot a look at Leonora, but her sister's expression made her falter and stop talking. "Leo?"

Leo, her mouth swollen from her injuries, couldn't look at her. "It's true," she whispered. "I wanted Jack for myself. I didn't think Paul was good enough for him—" She shot a look at the gun and gave a short, mirthless bark of laughter, "—and clearly I was right."

Noemi looked at her appalled. "You kept Jack from his father?"

She felt the gun being pressed against her temple. "Don't act like you didn't know, Noemi. It won't save your life."

Leo looked up at Paul. "She didn't know. I told her that you didn't want anything to do with us—with Jack. That you told me to get an abortion. That we meant nothing to you. Noemi didn't know. Nor did my parents."

The pressure on Noemi's temple fell away, and she saw Paul, unsure, staring at Leo. "She didn't know?"

"No one did. No one but me."

Paul and Leo stared at each other, then in a split second, Paul raised the gun and shot Leo in the head. Noemi screamed as her sister slumped onto her side, bleeding profusely, her eyes closed.

Paul grabbed Noemi and dragged her from the room, Noemi crying hysterically. He practically threw her down the stairs and, clamping a hand over her mouth, he hauled her out to Leo's car and threw her into the trunk.

"You're my insurance policy now, Noe. Once I'm out of the state..." He didn't finish his sentence, but she knew. She was a dead woman. Paul slammed the trunk closed, and she was in darkness.

As DREW DROVE, Rafa was on his phone calling the police, the FBI, everyone who could help them. He directed Drew to Leonora's house, but as they turned into her street, Rafa cursed. Leonora's car was speeding away from the house. "Follow her."

He knew if Leo had taken off that quickly, she had to have Noemi with her, or Noemi had already left. Leo was the key, the main target. Follow her; find Paul.

"Rafa... that's a guy driving that car. Sure it's Leonora's?"

Rafa felt ice cold fear in his veins. "Keep following them." Them? Somehow, he knew, he knew that this situation was bad. Noemi could be with him; both women could be in the car, both in danger...

...or Noemi could be lying dead at Leo's house. Rafa, calming himself despite his terror, called the police and gave them directions. "There could be... injured people." Don't say her name and she'll be okay....

They followed the other car for miles, Drew keeping up with it, and Rafa warning him not to alert the other driver to their presence. More and more his instinct told him Noemi was in that car.

The police called him back. "We have a shooting victim..."

His heart nearly broke in two. "A woman?"

"Yes. Shot in the head but she's alive. Caucasian, mid-thirties..."

Caucasian... Leo. Rafa knew he shouldn't be so relieved. "That's Leonora Castor. We're following her car, and I think the shooter has my girlfriend."

"Don't engage, sir! We're on our way."

Rafa ended the call. Don't engage. Yeah, right... if he had the chance to rescue his love, he wouldn't hesitate to engage.

"Rafa."

Drew indicated the car ahead which was swerving wildly now. Rafa leaned forward, and his heart soared as he saw Noemi wrapping her arms around Paul's head, trying to put him off, stop the car.

Oh, you good girl, you brave, brave girl. I'm here... I'm coming for you...

CHAPTER TWENTY-EIGHT

Noemi, trapped in the pitch-black trunk, calmed herself eventually and forced herself to think logically. Leo's car. She'd been in it a million times... The back seats were tricky. She could push them down, sneak into the backseat and...

She focused her thoughts entirely. She would wait until his speed picked up on a highway. He'd have to concentrate, so that when she burst through, he wouldn't have time to react. She had to get to his gun or the steering wheel before he did... if she could crash the car, they might stand a chance. She would curl into a ball, protect her babies as best she could.

It was either that or resign herself to a bullet. No. No way. No fucking way. She'd had her fill of hospital stays—her life was with Rafa and Bepi and her babies and being on the right side of the operating table now. This bastard wasn't going to stop her.

She counted down as she felt the car speed up. Ten... nine... eight...

As she reached one, she kicked out the seat behind the driver and threw herself through it. Paul gave a startled yelp as she wrapped her arms around his head, blinding him. He tried to steer with one hand; with the other, he yanked his gun from his pocket.

Noemi grabbed that hand and smashed it repeatedly against the stick shift until he screamed with pain and dropped the gun. "You fucking bitch!"

"You psycho motherfucker," she growled as she wrestled with him. "You killed my sister! You tried to kill me and my children! Fuck you! Fuck you, Paul!"

The car skidded and swerved and plowed through the fence at the side of the highway. Noemi clung onto Paul's head as the vehicle almost flew across a field and then, with a sickening crunch, it hit a tree, and Noemi was knocked unconscious.

"No! Noemi!" Rafa was beside himself as Drew drove through the broken fence towards the tree and the smoking wreck of Leo's car. Rafa was out and running before Drew even stopped his car.

As Rafa got to the car, he smelled gasoline. Panicking, he yanked open the backdoor and extracted Noemi's limp body. Paul was dead, his face mashed into the steering column, but Rafa couldn't give two fucks.

All his attention was on Noemi as he carried her away from the car, his eyes on her face as he willed her to be okay. Drew was waiting. "Get in the back seat with her. I'll drive us to the hospital."

Rafa lay Noemi gently on the back seat, then got in, settling her head on his lap. As Drew drove, Rafa stroked Noemi's hair. She didn't appear to have any injuries other than a bruised face and a cut above her ear, but she was so pale, so still. He pressed two fingers against her neck and was relieved that her pulse was so strong. "I love you so much, Noemi Castor. Please... open your eyes for me, baby."

He squeezed his own eyes shut then felt the slightest movement, then soft lips against his. "Hey, big guy." Her voice was gravelly, gruff, and soft. Rafa opened his eyes and saw her smile, her beautiful smile, and he couldn't help the tears that streamed down his face as the relief hit.

"Hey, beautiful girl..."

Her eyes filled with tears. "Is he dead? He killed Leo. He killed my sister!"

Rafa shook his head as he laid her gently on the ground, cradling her head. "No, darling. Leo's alive... she's holding on."

Noemi sighed. "Oh, thank God... thank God..."

"You better hang on, too, Noemi Castor." Rafa's voice shook and she smiled.

"I'm okay, just a little groggy." She touched his face. "Did you get even more handsome since this morning?"

Rafa chuckled, his emotions on the surface. "Noe... you are going to marry me, right?"

Noemi smiled, groggy, concussed but delighted to be alive. "I love you, Rafael Genova... but I gotta say... about damn time you asked."

Rafa laughed and kissed her. "I'm going to take that as a yes..."

"I might be concussed, so ask me again when I'm better."

Rafa winked at her. "And risk you saying no?"

"That, Rafa Genova, would never happen."

"Then tell me yes again and again."

Noemi smiled as she pulled his lips down to hers again. "Yes... yes... yes... yes..."

THE END.

ABOUT THE AUTHOR

Mrs. Love writes about smart, sexy women and the hot alpha billionaires who love them. She has found her own happily ever after with her dream husband and adorable 6 and 2 year old kids. Currently, Michelle is hard at work on the next book in the series, and trying to stay off the Internet.

"Thank you for supporting an indie author. Anything you can do, whether it be writing a review, or even simply telling a fellow reader that you enjoyed this. Thanks

❀ Created with Vellum